A Christmas Story

LOUIE BROWN

Copyright © 2024 by Louie Brown

Paperback: 978-1-965632-33-8
eBook: 978-1-965632-34-5
Library of Congress Control Number: 2024921001

All rights reserved. No part of this publication may be reproduced, distributed, or transmitted in any form or by any electronic or mechanical means, without the prior written permission of the publisher, except in the case of brief quotations embodied in critical reviews and certain other noncommercial uses permitted by copyright law.

This Book is a work of fiction. Names, characters, places, and incidents either are the product of the author's imagination or are used fictitiously. Any resemblance to actual persons, living or dead, events, or locales is entirely coincidental.

Ordering Information:

Prime Seven Media
518 Landmann St.
Tomah City, WI 54660

Printed in the United States of America

TABLE OF CONTENTS

Prologue 1

Chapter 1: No Guarantee 5

Chapter 2: The Poolside Heroics 10

Chapter 3: The Casson Family Tragedy 15

Chapter 4: Life in Foster Care 21

Chapter 5: Detective Sherlock Claus 27

Chapter 6: A Curious Discovery 36

Chapter 7: A New Path Forward 41

Chapter 8: A Family Secret Revealed 46

Chapter 9: A New Journey Begins 57

Chapter 10: A New Chapter Unfolds 71

Chapter 11: A Magical Journey 84

Chapter 12: A New Adventure Begins 96

Chapter 13: Unexpected Challenges 102

Chapter 14: The Big Night Approaches 111

Chapter 15: Christmas Magic 121

Epilogue 135

Prologue

*I*n a world where the extraordinary often hides behind the veil of the mundane, there are stories that weave together magic, loss, and the profound resilience of the human spirit. This is one such story—a tale that begins not with a flourish of grand adventures or magical epiphanies but with the simple yet profound existence of two little girls and their unwavering belief in a world where magic still holds sway.

It was a small town named Grahamvale, where everyone knew each other and where the rhythm of life was gentle and predictable. This town, with its cozy streets and well-worn paths, was a place where tales of heroism and tragedy were as familiar as the seasons themselves. Among the stories whispered and remembered, one tale stood out—a story of hope that had once shone brightly and was now destined to be rekindled.

At the heart of this tale were the Casson twins, Sandy and Suzie. From the moment they entered the world, their lives were destined to be intertwined with events that would shape not only their own futures but the future of those around them. Born to Charlie and Doris Casson, the twins were the apple of their parents' eyes. Charlie, a man of great warmth and skill, was known throughout Grahamvale for his craftsmanship and the love he poured into every piece of work he touched. Doris, equally adored, was the gentle heart of their family, her presence a soothing balm to those who knew her.

The Cassons were a family bound by more than just blood; they were united by their love for each other and their shared joy in simple pleasures. Their home was filled with laughter and love, and their workshop was a place where magical moments were crafted with every toy, every piece of furniture, and every act of kindness.

But life, as it often does, took a turn that was both cruel and swift. On a fateful Christmas Eve, tragedy struck the Casson family with a brutal force. Doris and the twins' unborn sister were taken from them in a tragic car accident, leaving Charlie to face the unthinkable. He was left to shoulder the weight of his grief while trying to be both mother and father to his beloved twins. In the midst of his sorrow, Charlie continued to teach Sandy and Suzie the values of resilience, kindness, and the importance of seeing the magic in the world around them.

Yet, as if fate had more in store for them, Charlie too was taken, succumbing to a heart attack in his workshop, the place where he had spent countless hours shaping not only wood but the very essence of his family's spirit. The news was delivered with a heavy heart by Dr. Camilo Guerra, a family friend who had known the Cassons for years. The loss was overwhelming, and Sandy and Suzie were left to navigate their grief, clinging to the lessons their father had imparted.

In the wake of their parents' deaths, the twins were placed into foster care—a transition that brought them into the homes of two very different couples. Sandy was taken in by the Mallorys, an older, distant couple who provided stability but little warmth. Suzie, meanwhile, found herself with the Nielsens, a younger couple who seemed more affectionate but whose household held an undercurrent of unease. Despite their close proximity, the separation was a painful divide, one that was made bearable only by the rare weekends they could spend together.

It wasn't long before Sandy and Suzie discovered unsettling truths about their new guardians. The Mallorys and the Nielsens, it seemed, were entangled in activities far from the benign façade they presented. As the twins uncovered evidence of illicit dealings, their feelings of betrayal and fear grew. Their attempts to seek help led them to Officer Morales, a local cop who promised to investigate discreetly while advising them to remain vigilant and maintain their cover.

Their search for justice and a sense of normalcy led them to act out in ways that were far from their intentions. Driven by their experiences and a desire to make a difference, they embarked on their own risky venture—returning stolen goods to those in need, inspired by a sense of justice that was both naive and courageous. However, their activities caught the attention of the authorities, leading to a confrontation with the law.

Just when their future seemed uncertain, the twins encountered a figure who would alter the course of their lives. Detective Sherlock Claus—a whimsical yet wise character—stepped into their lives, offering them a new path. Claus, with his magical air and profound understanding, revealed that he had been watching over them, noting their trials and their remarkable potential. He introduced them to their father's legacy and offered them a chance to continue his work in a way that combined their father's teachings with their own spirit of giving.

As the story unfolds, Sandy and Suzie embark on a journey filled with magic, mystery, and a renewed sense of purpose. Guided by Claus and aided by a network of helpers, they dive into the world of toy repair and charitable work, discovering that the magic of their father's legacy is not just about fixing broken objects but about mending the world around them. Their adventure becomes one of personal growth, community involvement, and a deepened understanding of the true spirit of Christmas.

Chapter 1

No Guarantee

Rudy leaned against the doorframe of Nick's cluttered office, his broad shoulders barely fitting in the narrow entrance. The room was a study in organized chaos, with shelves overflowing with old tomes, curious trinkets, and bits of mechanical parts, giving the place an air of timelessness. Every inch of the space was a testament to a life well-lived, filled with centuries of memories.

A collection of antique chairs stood haphazardly in one corner, their creaky frames showing the wear of many years, while a large desk—covered in half-finished toys, brass gears, and fading papers—dominated the center. Despite the mess, Rudy's towering presence made it feel as though the room had shrunk.

At 6 feet 4 inches, Rudy was an imposing figure, built like a sturdy oak. His red nose, glowing like a winter beacon, was his most distinctive feature—a result of years spent working in the freezing winds of the northern forests, where snowstorms were a constant companion. It gave him an almost mythical quality, though in truth, Rudy's presence alone was enough to demand respect.

"Nick," Rudy's deep voice cut through the silence, its usual jovial tone replaced with concern, "do you have a moment?"

Nick, seated behind his overflowing desk, didn't immediately respond. He was polishing an old pair of spectacles, his silvery beard catching the soft light from the overhead lamp. Nick was an enigma.

His appearance suggested an age that no one could quite place—his wisdom surpassed time, and there was an ageless quality about him. He was both youthful and ancient, a paradox of energy and experience. Though no one could say for sure, there was a sense that Nick had seen centuries pass as easily as a man might watch the seasons change.

After a pause, Nick finally glanced up, his keen eyes locking onto Rudy. He set down his spectacles and, with a wave of his hand, invited Rudy in. "Of course. Come in, my friend."

Rudy stepped into the office, the wooden floor groaning under the weight of his heavy boots. There was something different in his manner today, a kind of seriousness that hadn't been there in their previous conversations. He approached Nick's desk, leaning in slightly as if the subject he was about to broach needed the intimacy of lowered voices.

"Have you made a decision about the next project? More importantly, have you decided who's going to lead it?"

Nick's eyes softened, and he stood up slowly, straightening his vest before sliding the spectacles onto his face. He was considerably shorter than Rudy, but that didn't matter—Nick's presence was every bit as commanding. With a thoughtful look, he gestured for Rudy to follow him. "Let's take a walk."

They exited the office and stepped into the sprawling workshop, an awe-inspiring sight that never failed to impress. It was a vast, industrial space, humming with life and energy. Rows upon rows of elves, dressed in green overalls and bright red belts, were hard at work—hammering, painting, crafting.

The rhythmic sound of machinery filled the air, while the smell of wood shavings and fresh paint hung thick around them. Shelves were packed with materials of every kind—colored papers, paints, tools—everything one could imagine needed to make the most beautiful toys.

It was a place of creation, where magic came to life.

Nick and Rudy walked in silence for a while, the workshop's noise filling the space between them. Eventually, they stopped near a group of elves who were carefully writing in large leather-bound ledgers, their quills moving quickly as they recorded the deeds of children from all over the world—keeping track of who had been good and who had been bad.

Nick broke the silence first, his voice measured and thoughtful. "Rudy, I've been watching a pair of twins for the past nine years. Their names are Sandy and Suzie."

Rudy's thick eyebrows furrowed in curiosity. "Twins? What makes them so important?"

Nick turned to face Rudy, his eyes gleaming with excitement. "They've faced hardship, more than most children their age, yet they've never lost their belief in magic. Even now, when the world is so full of disbelief, they still cling to that hope. They've held on to something most children lose far too soon."

Rudy's skepticism was evident. "Kids who believe in magic? Sure, that's rare. But what makes them worth the risk? What makes them different from the others?"

Nick's expression grew more serious. "These children... they've seen things no child should see. They've lost their parents, been thrown into a world that's unkind and unforgiving. But instead of letting that darkness consume them, they've held on to kindness, to imagination. It's more than just belief, Rudy. They have the potential to change everything."

Rudy shook his head slightly. "Potential's a dangerous thing, Nick. You know that. It's unpredictable."

Nick nodded in agreement. "Yes, it is. There are no guarantees. Magic... even for me, it's not always reliable. But there's something special about these twins. They're standing at a crossroads. If we guide them, they could achieve greatness. But if we don't... well, they could lose that magic forever."

The weight of Nick's words settled over them both. Rudy stared at the bustling workshop, watching as toys were carefully assembled, each piece falling into place with precision. He understood the stakes now. This wasn't just about toys or even the next project—it was about something far more important.

"So, we're taking a gamble on them," Rudy said, his tone cautious.

Nick smiled faintly. "A gamble worth taking. They've been through so much, yet they remain unbroken. If we can help them realize their potential, they could become something extraordinary."

For a long moment, the two men stood in silence, the clatter of the workshop fading into the background. Finally, Rudy spoke, his voice low and thoughtful. "I'll need to see them for myself. I need to know if they're really what you think they are."

Nick's smile widened, his eyes twinkling with understanding. "I thought you might say that. We'll arrange for a meeting. You'll see what I mean."

Rudy nodded, satisfied for now. He turned to leave, his boots echoing on the wooden floor as he headed toward the exit. But before he could step outside, Nick called after him, his voice softer, more contemplative.

"Rudy, remember… we're not just shaping toys. We're shaping the future."

Rudy paused at the doorway, the weight of Nick's words hanging in the air like a thick mist. He turned slightly, just enough to give Nick a firm nod before walking out into the snowy landscape beyond the workshop.

The snow had started to fall more heavily now, blanketing the forest in a quiet, serene layer of white. Somewhere out there, two children—Sandy and Suzie—were living their lives, unaware of the destiny that awaited them. Unaware of the magic that would soon change their lives forever.

As Rudy walked deeper into the pine forest, his mind whirled with thoughts of the twins and the unknown future ahead. It was a gamble, yes. But something in Nick's voice, in the way he spoke of those children, made Rudy believe that maybe—just maybe—this was a gamble worth taking.

There were no guarantees in magic, no promises of success. But for the first time in a long while, Rudy felt something stir deep within him: hope.

Chapter 2

THE POOLSIDE HEROICS

Nick leaned back in his chair, the corners of his mouth lifting into a small smile as his eyes flickered with warmth. The room seemed to fade away, leaving only the vivid memory of a day long past. "It was twelve years ago," he began, his voice calm but rich with nostalgia.

"A scorching summer afternoon in Grahamvale—the kind of heat that makes everything slow down. You could feel it in the air, heavy and still, pressing down on everything. Even the trees seemed tired, their leaves drooping as if they were surrendering to the heat."

Nick paused, letting the scene settle in the room like a soft haze. "The Casson family was there that day at the public pool. Frank, Doris, and their twins—Sandy and Suzie. They were just little ones then, barely three years old.

But you wouldn't have known it from the way they moved in the water. They swam like little fish, completely at ease, darting through the shallow end with so much energy and joy. Their parents watched them with pride, as parents do. But even then, there was something about those twins that stood out, even if no one could quite put their finger on it."

Rudy, who had been listening in silence, leaned in slightly, his interest piqued. There was a subtle curiosity in his gaze, but he remained quiet, waiting for Nick to continue. Nick, his eyes now distant as if he were reliving that summer day, resumed his story.

"The public pool was the heart of Grahamvale in the summer. Everyone in town went there to escape the heat, to cool off, and to forget about life's troubles for a while. It was one of those days where the place was packed. Families everywhere—blankets and towels spread across the grass, kids running around, their laughter filling the air. You could smell sunscreen, feel the cool mist of water in the breeze, and hear the soft splashes of kids jumping into the pool."

Nick's voice took on a subtle intensity as he continued. "At one end of the pool, the older kids—teenagers—were tossing a beach ball back and forth, their shouts echoing in the heavy air. At the other end, closer to the shallow part, Sandy and Suzie were splashing around, laughing and playing like any other kids. Their parents were close by, keeping an eye on them, but it was such a relaxed atmosphere that no one could have imagined anything would go wrong."

But, of course, things did go wrong.

"Unbeknownst to almost everyone there, a toddler—Nathan—had wandered away from his parents. He was a big boy for his age, but still not steady on his feet. He was only a few feet away from the deep end of the pool, drawn to the noise and energy of the older kids. No one noticed him. His parents were distracted, talking with friends, assuming he was safe playing nearby. But toddlers are quick, and the next thing anyone knew, he was teetering dangerously close to the water's edge."

Nick's expression grew more serious. "But someone did notice—Suzie. From the shallow end, where she had been playing with Sandy, she saw Nathan. And something inside her just…knew. Without hesitating, she grabbed Sandy by the arm, and the two of them made their way toward the deep end. They didn't shout, didn't scream for help. Their parents, Frank and Doris, probably thought they were just wandering off to explore the pool."

Nick paused again, letting the tension build. "No one else saw Nathan stumble. His little foot slipped on the wet concrete at the edge of the pool, and suddenly, he was in the water. His body hit the surface with a small splash—so small that none of the older kids playing nearby even noticed. But Suzie and Sandy did. Without a moment's hesitation, Suzie dove in after him. She didn't think about the fact that she was only three years old, or that the water was much deeper than she was used to. She just knew she had to help."

Rudy shifted in his seat, clearly engrossed in the story. "They were just kids," he murmured, more to himself than to Nick.

Nick nodded in agreement, his eyes thoughtful. "Yes, just kids. But there was something special about them, even then."

As Nick continued, his voice softened, full of admiration. "Sandy was right behind her sister, and together, they swam toward Nathan. He was panicking by this point, his little arms flailing as he struggled to stay above the water. The twins reached him just in time. Suzie got to him first, wrapping her arms around him, while Sandy helped pull him toward the side of the pool. Their small bodies worked in unison, and despite their age, they managed to lift Nathan out of the water and onto the pool's edge."

Nick paused, letting the scene settle. "By the time Frank realized something was wrong and rushed over, it was already done. His two little girls, barely old enough to be out of diapers, had saved a life. Nathan was coughing and crying, but he was safe, thanks to them."

There was a moment of silence between Nick and Rudy. The weight of the story hung in the air. Then, Nick smiled again, the pride unmistakable in his voice. "Word spread quickly, of course. Within hours, everyone in town knew what the Casson twins had done. They were hailed as heroes. The local paper ran a story about it the next day—'Toddler Saved by Local Twins at Grahamvale Pool.' Everyone talked about how brave they were, how calm and quick-thinking. But that wasn't the whole story."

Rudy raised an eyebrow, intrigued. "What do you mean?"

Nick's smile faded slightly, his tone becoming more serious. "That day at the pool was just the beginning. What made Sandy and Suzie special wasn't just what they did that day—it was what they became after. That day, they showed the world a glimpse of who they really were, but their story didn't end with saving Nathan. In fact, it was only the first chapter of a much bigger story."

Rudy leaned back, digesting Nick's words. "So, saving that boy—it was a sign of things to come?"

Nick nodded, his eyes distant once more. "Exactly. There was something in them, something beyond the ordinary. That day at the pool wasn't just about two kids being in the right place at the right time. It was about destiny. Sandy and Suzie were meant for something greater, even if they didn't know it yet. The bravery they showed that day was a spark, a small glimpse of what they were capable of."

Nick's voice softened, as if speaking more to himself now than to Rudy. "Life has a way of testing people, of pushing them to their limits. And those two—they've faced tests far harder than that day at the pool. But even now, all these years later, I can still see that spark in them. That same courage, that same determination. It's what makes them different. It's what makes them special."

Rudy was quiet for a long moment, lost in thought. Then he looked up at Nick, his expression thoughtful. "You think they're ready for what's coming?"

Nick's gaze was steady, but there was a flicker of uncertainty in his eyes. "I think they've always been ready. They just need to realize it."

The room fell silent again, the story of that hot summer day lingering between them like a half-forgotten memory. Outside, the world continued to move forward, but in that small room, time seemed to stand still, caught in the echo of a past that was far from over.

Chapter 3

THE CASSON FAMILY TRAGEDY

Charlie Casson was a man whose quiet strength and unwavering dedication left an indelible mark on the small community of Grahamvale. Known for his craftsmanship, Charlie was much more than just a tradesman. His skills ranged from renovating homes to repairing toys, but his true gift was the way he touched the lives of those around him.

Everyone knew that if they needed help—whether it was a leaky roof or a broken doll—Charlie would lend a hand, often refusing to accept more than a heartfelt "thank you" in return. Yet, it wasn't just his work that earned him respect. It was the love and devotion he showed to his family, especially to his twin children, Sandy and Suzie.

Charlie's workshop was a cherished space, filled with the sounds of hammering and the smell of fresh sawdust. It was more than just a place to earn a living; it was where he passed down the values he held most dear. Sandy and Suzie had been his constant companions in the workshop ever since they were old enough to hold a hammer.

For Charlie, teaching them to repair broken things was about more than just showing them a useful skill—it was about instilling in them the importance of kindness, patience, and putting care into everything they did. He had a saying he would often repeat with a twinkle in his eye: "Always add a little something extra." Whether it was an extra coat of polish on a piece of furniture or a small, personal note of thanks, Charlie believed that going the extra mile was what truly mattered.

However, the warmth of their family home concealed a deep and lingering wound. Two years earlier, on a fateful Christmas Eve, tragedy had struck the Casson family. Doris, Charlie's beloved wife, was heavily pregnant and just days away from giving birth to their third child. It was supposed to be a joyous time, a new beginning for their growing family. But in an instant, their happiness was shattered.

As they were driving to the hospital during a snowstorm, their car was struck by a speeding driver who had lost control on the icy roads. The impact was devastating. Doris and their unborn baby were killed instantly, while Sandy and Suzie, who were only ten years old at the time, survived the crash physically unscathed. But emotionally, they were never the same.

The loss of their mother left a gaping hole in their hearts. Doris had been the anchor of their family, her warmth and nurturing spirit a constant source of comfort. Her absence was keenly felt in every corner of the home. The twins struggled to comprehend a world without her, and though they were surrounded by friends and neighbors offering their support, nothing could fill the void.

For Charlie, the grief was almost unbearable. Losing Doris and their unborn child on Christmas Eve, a night that should have been filled with hope and anticipation, was a cruel twist of fate. Yet, despite the immense pain he carried, Charlie knew he had to keep going—for Sandy and Suzie's sake.

Charlie threw himself into his role as both father and mother to the twins. Every day, he worked tirelessly to ensure that their lives continued as normally as possible. He woke up early to cook their breakfast, helped them with their homework, and brought them into the workshop every afternoon to keep their minds occupied. For a while, it seemed like life was moving forward. The twins were excelling in school, and they cherished the time they spent learning their father's trade. But beneath the surface, they were all still grieving.

Charlie's grief was something he kept hidden, locked away beneath his calm demeanor. He never let the twins see the depth of his sorrow, always smiling, always patient. He wanted to protect them from his pain, to shield them from the darkness that weighed so heavily on his heart. But without Doris, the light that had once filled their home had dimmed. Each day felt like an uphill battle, and though Charlie continued to be the rock for his children, the weight of his loss was growing heavier with each passing day.

Then came the day that changed everything.

It was a crisp autumn afternoon, and Charlie was alone in his workshop, working on an old bicycle that had come in for repair. The sun was setting, casting a golden light through the windows, and the familiar scent of pine shavings filled the air. The rhythmic sound of his tools echoed through the shop as he tightened the last bolt on the bike's frame.

But just as he was about to move on to the next task, a sharp, searing pain shot through his chest. It radiated down his left arm, leaving him gasping for breath. He dropped the wrench he was holding, the metallic clang of it hitting the floor reverberating in the quiet room.

Charlie knew something was terribly wrong.

His first instinct was to reach for the phone and call his best friend, Dr. Camilo Guerra. Camilo had been Charlie's closest confidant for years, a doctor whose wisdom and friendship had seen the Casson family through many trials. But when Charlie dialed his number, there was no answer. Camilo was in the middle of an appointment, unavailable for just a few more crucial minutes. Charlie's breathing grew labored as the pain intensified. He stumbled toward his desk and collapsed into his chair, his heart pounding wildly in his chest.

With trembling hands, Charlie grabbed a scrap of paper and a pencil. He scribbled down a single word: "Dot." It was the nickname he had called Doris for as long as they had been together. Writing it was his way of reaching out to her, as if, in his final moments, he wanted to be close to the woman he had loved so deeply and lost so tragically. Beside her name, he drew a small smiley face, a final, simple gesture of affection—a goodbye filled with the same warmth and care he had shown throughout his life.

When Dr. Guerra finally returned the call, it was too late.

Camilo rushed to the workshop as soon as he could, his heart heavy with dread. As he pushed open the door, he was met with a sight that would haunt him for the rest of his days. Charlie sat slumped in his chair, his hand still loosely gripping the pencil. The small piece of paper with Doris's name lay on the desk in front of him, a quiet testament to the love that had endured even in death.

For a long, agonizing moment, the only sound in the room was the slow, steady ticking of the workshop clock, each second a painful reminder of the fragility of life. Camilo stood frozen, overcome with guilt and sorrow. He had missed Charlie's call. He had been too late. But as a doctor, he knew in his heart that even if he had arrived on time, there was nothing he could have done. Charlie's heart had given out long before help could reach him.

After making the necessary calls to the authorities, Camilo faced the hardest task of all: telling Sandy and Suzie that their father was gone. He called their school, his voice unsteady as he asked the principal to send them home early. The principal, sensing the gravity of the situation, agreed without hesitation. When the twins arrived at the workshop, still in their school uniforms and laughing over some joke they had shared on the walk home, the sight of Camilo waiting for them with a police officer by his side immediately wiped the smiles from their faces.

"Where's Dad?" Suzie asked, her voice trembling as she clutched the straps of her backpack.

Camilo knelt in front of her, his heart breaking as he looked into her wide, innocent eyes. "I'm so sorry, Suzie. Your dad... he's gone."

Sandy, standing beside his sister, paled. His hands balled into fists, his body stiff with denial. "No," he whispered, shaking his head. "No, he can't be. He's fine. He's... he's fine."

But no amount of denial could change the truth. In the span of just two years, the Casson twins had lost both their mother and their father. Their world, once filled with love, warmth, and security, had crumbled, leaving them standing in the wreckage of their childhood.

For Suzie, the loss was like being cast adrift in a storm, her sense of safety and stability torn away. She collapsed into Camilo's arms, sobbing uncontrollably as waves of grief crashed over her. But for Sandy, something else stirred deep within him. He felt the weight of responsibility settle on his young shoulders, the realization that, with both of their parents gone, he would have to be the one to protect his sister. He would have to be strong, even though the grief threatened to consume him.

As the sun set on that terrible day, the Casson twins stood hand in hand outside their father's workshop, their lives forever changed. But even in the midst of their despair, the lessons Charlie had taught them—the values of resilience, kindness, and hard work—remained. Though they were just children, those lessons would carry them through the darkest of times, guiding them as they navigated the uncertain path that lay ahead.

Chapter 4

LIFE IN FOSTER CARE

After the devastating death of their father, Sandy and Suzie Casson found themselves thrust into an unimaginable reality—one marked by the absence of family and the cold, impersonal structure of foster care. At just twelve years old, they were separated from each other, suddenly thrust into a world devoid of the love and familiarity they had once taken for granted.

The immediate aftermath of their father's death was a whirlwind of grief and uncertainty. The twins, who had always been inseparable, were now faced with the daunting challenge of navigating a life that had been turned upside down. The loss of Charlie Casson, their beloved father, was a blow they could hardly comprehend. He had been their rock, their guide, and the center of their small, tight-knit world. Now, with him gone, they were left to grapple with a new and frightening reality.

Dr. Camilo Guerra and his wife Trish, the closest friends of Charlie and Doris, had been the natural choice to take in the twins. Camilo, who had been a confidant and adviser to Charlie, had been the one to deliver the heart-wrenching news of their father's passing. In the midst of their mourning, Camilo and Trish had stepped forward, eager to provide the stability and care that Sandy and Suzie so desperately needed.

However, fate was unkind. Trish's health, already precarious for years, had worsened significantly. The couple's heartfelt attempt to adopt the twins was met with resistance from the state authorities, who, concerned for Trish's deteriorating condition, deemed them unfit to provide the care Sandy and Suzie required.

This rejection was a crushing blow to the twins, who had hoped that their closest family friends would offer them a semblance of normalcy. Though Camilo and Trish could not become their legal guardians, they vowed to remain a steady presence in their lives, offering what support and love they could.

Despite these efforts, the absence of a stable home and the emotional upheaval left the twins in a state of deep disarray. The state placed Sandy and Suzie into separate foster homes, a decision that only compounded their sense of abandonment. Though their new homes were relatively close to each other, the emotional distance between them felt immeasurable. The state's intention to keep them nearby in an effort to mitigate their pain proved futile; each day spent apart was a reminder of the family they had lost and the life they once knew.

Sandy was placed with the Mallorys, an elderly couple who lived on the outskirts of town. Their home, a grand and pristine house, felt more like a museum than a residence. The Mallorys, though well-meaning, provided Sandy with the necessities—clothes, food, and a private room—but their kindness was laced with formality.

Their interactions with Sandy were marked by polite distance and impersonal gestures. There was no warmth in their home, no sense of familial belonging. The atmosphere was stifling, and Sandy often found himself staring out of his bedroom window, feeling as though he were adrift in a vast, uncharted sea. The clouds outside seemed to mirror his sense of floating through life, untethered and alone.

Suzie, meanwhile, was placed with the Nielsens, a younger couple living only a few miles from the Mallorys. The Nielsens' home, though closer in age to the twins, had its own set of challenges.

Mrs. Nielsen, despite her efforts to engage Suzie in activities and conversations, could not dispel the underlying sense of unease that settled over Suzie. There was a palpable tension in the house, an unsettling feeling that the Nielsens' outward friendliness was merely a facade. Suzie often sensed an unspoken discomfort, a gnawing doubt that something was amiss.

Adjusting to their new lives proved to be a Herculean task. The twins missed the comforting routine of their father's workshop and the safety of their previous home. Weekends became their sanctuary—a precious respite from the cold and unfamiliar world of foster care.

They would meet at a small park near the river, a rare green space where they could converse freely and momentarily escape their solitary existences. These meetings were a lifeline, a reminder of their shared bond amidst the turmoil of their separate lives.

As time passed, however, the twins began to sense an unsettling shift. Initially, it was a vague feeling—a gnawing awareness that something was not quite right. The Mallorys and the Nielsens often held secretive meetings, their gatherings shrouded in mystery and conducted behind closed doors. These meetings, always occurring late into the night, were explained away as "adult business," but the secrecy left Sandy and Suzie uneasy and curious.

Sandy, ever observant, started noticing odd behaviors in the Mallory household. Mr. Mallory would take phone calls in the dead of night, his voice hushed and guarded. Mrs. Mallory frequently left the house for hours without providing clear explanations, and when Sandy inquired about her whereabouts, she offered vague and unsatisfactory answers. Though Sandy initially tried to dismiss these occurrences as mere quirks of his new environment, the increasing frequency and peculiarity of these behaviors made them impossible to ignore.

At the Nielsen residence, Suzie observed similar patterns. Mr. Nielsen would engage in intense, whispered phone conversations, abruptly ending them whenever Suzie entered the room. Mrs. Nielsen, despite her outwardly warm demeanor, often appeared distracted and preoccupied, her thoughts seemingly elsewhere even when she was physically present. Suzie's growing suspicion that their foster parents were hiding something created a constant undercurrent of anxiety.

The turning point came one weekend when both sets of foster parents abruptly left town, leaving Sandy and Suzie alone in their respective homes. Although the twins had been left unsupervised before, this time there was no explanation for their absence, no mention of when they would return. This lack of transparency fueled Sandy's determination to uncover the truth.

With the Mallorys away, Sandy seized the opportunity to investigate. He searched their house thoroughly, driven by a growing sense of urgency. It wasn't long before he stumbled upon a locked drawer in Mr. Mallory's office. Inside, he found a collection of documents—bank statements, legal papers, and ledgers.

As he scanned the pages, his heart pounded. The documents detailed transactions involving offshore accounts, significant sums of money being transferred, and references to enigmatic "clients." It was evident that the

Mallorys were involved in illegal activities far beyond what Sandy had anticipated.

The next day, at their usual meeting spot in the park, Sandy shared his findings with Suzie. As they sat on their favorite bench, Suzie revealed that she had discovered similar documents at the Nielsens' home. Together, they pieced together a disturbing picture: their foster parents were colluding in illegal activities, possibly involving money laundering or fraud. The gravity of this revelation was overwhelming, and the weight of their newfound knowledge was suffocating.

"We need to tell someone," Suzie said, her voice trembling with fear and urgency. The thought of exposing their foster parents felt perilous, yet their silence seemed equally dangerous.

Sandy, ever cautious, shook his head. "We don't have enough proof yet. If we go to the authorities without concrete evidence, we could end up in serious trouble ourselves. We need to gather more information before taking any action."

Reluctantly, Suzie agreed, though fear continued to gnaw at her. The twins resolved to maintain their façade of obedient foster children while continuing their investigation. Each day felt like a precarious balancing act, fraught with the risk of discovery.

Weeks passed, and the twins became adept at covert operations. They eavesdropped on conversations, followed their foster parents, and collected any scrap of information they could find. But the deeper they dug, the more dangerous their situation became. Sandy noticed that Mr. Mallory's suspicions were growing; he began asking Sandy increasingly probing questions. Suzie also felt the Nielsens' scrutiny intensify, their eyes watching her more closely.

Realizing the gravity of their predicament, the twins decided to seek help. They reached out to Officer Morales, a local police officer who had shown kindness to their father in the past. Morales had always looked out for them in small ways, and they trusted him more than anyone else.

One rainy afternoon, while their foster parents were away, the twins met Morales in the park. They laid bare the entire situation—the documents, the secret meetings, and the suspicious behaviors. Morales listened attentively, his expression growing more serious with each detail. "You did the right thing coming to me," he said, his voice steady and reassuring. "But you need to be cautious. If these people are involved in illegal activities, they could be dangerous. I'll handle the investigation from here. In the meantime, keep your heads down and don't let them know you're onto them."

Relieved yet still anxious, the twins returned to their foster homes, their hope resting on Morales' ability to uncover the truth before it was too late. They continued to play their roles as model foster children while living under the constant shadow of fear.

Little did they know that their lives were on the verge of another unexpected twist—one that would test their courage and resilience in ways they could never have imagined.

Chapter 5
Detective Sherlock Claus

Life in foster care had hardened Sandy and Suzie, turning their childhood into a blur of responsibilities and losses. At sixteen, they had experienced more than many people twice their age. The death of their parents, the secrets hidden behind the walls of their foster homes, and the lingering pain of feeling abandoned had aged them prematurely.

While other teenagers were concerned with school, friends, and hobbies, the twins were entangled in a world of grief, uncertainty, and suspicion. Yet, even with the weight of their past resting on their shoulders, nothing could have prepared them for the arrival of the strange figure who was about to enter their lives and change their world forever.

It was an especially cold winter morning, the kind that made every breath feel sharp. Suzie stood in the kitchen, half-awake, making herself a cup of tea. She had pulled on the oversized sweater she wore to fend off the morning chill.

The house was quiet except for the soft sound of the kettle heating on the stove. Sandy, ever the early riser, sat by the living room window. His gaze was fixed on the frost-covered yard outside, where the trees stood like icy sculptures. His thoughts drifted between memories of their parents and the gnawing suspicion that something wasn't right with their foster parents.

Suddenly, the shrill sound of the doorbell pierced the quiet morning. It startled Suzie, causing her to spill some tea. She cursed under her breath and quickly wiped up the mess with a dish towel. Sandy didn't move at first, his mind still lost in thought. It wasn't until the doorbell rang again that he snapped out of his daze and walked over to answer it.

When Sandy opened the door, he was met with a sight so unusual that he blinked, unsure if he was still daydreaming. Standing before him was a man who looked as though he had wandered out of another time, or perhaps another world entirely. He was stout and dressed in a thick, old-fashioned wool coat that nearly brushed the ground.

His beard was long and snow-white, flowing down to his chest, and his eyes, a bright, twinkling blue, sparkled with a mischievous warmth. Everything about him, from his appearance to his mannerisms, seemed out of place, like a character pulled from a fairy tale or a Christmas card.

"Good morning, Sandy," the man said, his voice deep and filled with a strange energy. "I've been waiting a long time to meet you and your sister."

Sandy stared, his hand still on the door handle. He had no idea how to respond. Before he could say a word, Suzie appeared behind him, holding her cup of tea, a confused expression on her face.

"Who is it?" she asked, looking at the stranger with suspicion.

The man smiled and gave a small bow, tipping his worn hat as he introduced himself. "I'm Sherlock Claus," he said, the name rolling off his tongue as if it were the most natural thing in the world. "I know this is quite unexpected, but I've come to help you."

Suzie's brow furrowed, and she instinctively tightened her grip on the cup. "Help us? With what?"

Without waiting for an invitation, the man stepped inside, closing the door behind him as though he had been invited all along. His presence filled the room, commanding attention, yet oddly enough, it wasn't threatening. Despite her apprehension, Suzie couldn't help but feel a strange sense of comfort radiating from him. Sandy, on the other hand, was less convinced. His eyes followed the man's every move, and he crossed his arms defensively.

Sherlock Claus, seemingly unbothered by the tension, glanced around the modest living room. His twinkling eyes took in every detail, as if he had been there before. When he turned back to the twins, his expression softened, and his voice took on a more serious tone.

"You've been through more than any child should," he began, looking at each of them in turn. "Losing your parents, dealing with the strange and dangerous lives of your foster families… I know it's been hard. But there's something important you need to know—something about your future."

Sandy narrowed his eyes, his suspicion deepening. "How do you know all that? Who are you really?"

Sherlock Claus chuckled softly, his blue eyes gleaming. "I'm exactly who I say I am, Sandy. Sherlock Claus. I've been watching over you both for quite some time now. And I know that your parents left behind more than just memories—they left behind a legacy. And now, that legacy belongs to you."

Suzie exchanged a glance with Sandy, her own skepticism reflected in her brother's expression. "What kind of legacy?" she asked, her voice wary.

Sherlock Claus reached into his coat and pulled out a weathered leather-bound notebook. The edges of the cover were frayed, and the pages inside looked yellowed and fragile. He handed it to Suzie with a gentle smile.

"This," he said softly, "belonged to your father."

Suzie's eyes widened as she carefully took the notebook from him. Her fingers brushed over the worn leather, and she felt a pang of emotion. It was like holding a piece of her father, something she thought she would never have again. Slowly, she opened the notebook and saw her father's familiar handwriting, the ink faded but still legible.

"He wasn't just a craftsman," Sherlock Claus continued. "Your father believed in fixing what was broken—not just toys or objects, but people too. He spread kindness through his work, offering help to those who couldn't afford new things. He believed in second chances, in mending hearts as much as he mended toys."

Sandy leaned closer, his skepticism slowly giving way to curiosity. "And what does that have to do with us?" he asked, his voice still guarded.

Sherlock Claus's smile deepened. "Your father's legacy doesn't end with him. It's your turn now, Sandy. Suzie. You've both been through incredible hardships, but you've come out stronger because of them. And now, you have the opportunity to carry on his work—not just repairing toys, but bringing hope to people who need it most. That's why I'm here. To guide you. To help you realize the potential your father always saw in you."

The room was silent for a moment, the weight of Sherlock Claus's words hanging in the air. Suzie, still clutching the notebook, felt a strange mixture of hope and uncertainty. "What if we don't want to carry on his legacy?" she asked, her voice quieter now. "What if we're not ready?"

Sherlock Claus's expression softened further. "That's for you to decide," he said gently. "But remember this—your father believed in you. He knew that you had something special, something the world needs. This isn't just about fixing toys. It's about reminding people that even in the darkest times, there's still light to be found."

Sandy uncrossed his arms, his defenses slowly crumbling. "If we do this," he asked, his voice serious, "how do we even start? We don't have a workshop. We don't have the tools or the skills."

A twinkle returned to Sherlock Claus's eyes as he smiled. "Leave that to me," he said. "Your father's workshop still stands, and I've made sure that it's ready for you. Everything you need is already there. As for the skills, well, I'll be here to teach you. Just as your father would have."

Suzie looked down at the notebook again, feeling the weight of her father's legacy. It was overwhelming, yet somehow, for the first time in a long time, she didn't feel alone. "And what about our foster parents?" she asked quietly. "They're involved in some dangerous things. If we stay with them..."

Sherlock Claus's smile turned slightly mischievous, his eyes gleaming with something that almost resembled amusement. "Let me handle that," he said. "There are forces at work beyond what you've seen, Suzie. You're not alone in this. Things are already being set in motion to protect you. All you need to focus on is what's in front of you."

As he spoke, Claus turned toward the door, preparing to leave. But before he stepped outside, he paused and looked back at the twins one last time. His expression was soft and filled with a deep sincerity. "Remember," he said, "your father saw the best in you both. And so do I. The world needs people like you now more than ever."

With that, Sherlock Claus stepped out into the cold, snowy morning, disappearing as mysteriously as he had arrived. Suzie and Sandy stood frozen in the doorway, watching the empty street, their minds swirling with everything they had just heard.

"What just happened?" Sandy muttered, still trying to process everything.

"I don't know," Suzie replied, her voice filled with wonder as she flipped through the pages of the notebook. "But I think... we just got our second chance."

Outside, the snow began to fall softly, each flake drifting gently from the sky. Inside, for the first time in years, the twins felt a flicker of hope. Whatever lay ahead, they knew they wouldn't face it alone. They had each other, the memory of their father, and the guidance of the strange but kind man who called himself Sherlock Claus.

As Sandy and Suzie stood in the doorway, the world outside seemed to transform. The cold winter air carried the promise of change, and the sight of the snow-covered street felt like a blank slate, waiting to be filled with new possibilities. They stared at the empty space where Claus had disappeared, the impact of his visit settling over them like the snow on the ground.

"It's like... he brought a piece of our past back to life," Suzie said quietly, her fingers still tracing the faded ink of their father's notebook.

Sandy nodded, his usual skepticism giving way to a cautious optimism. "It's hard to believe, but there's something about him... something real. Maybe this is what we needed all along."

They turned back into the house, the warmth from the heater a stark contrast to the chill outside. The small living room, filled with the mundane clutter of everyday life, now seemed like the setting for something much larger. The old furniture, the mismatched curtains, and the half-empty shelves all felt like a stage waiting for the next act.

Suzie sat down on the worn-out couch, placing the notebook on her lap. She opened it again, letting her eyes wander over the pages filled with her father's handwriting. Each entry was a reminder of the kindness and hope he had spread, a legacy they were now called to continue.

Sandy paced the room, his mind racing with the possibilities Claus had hinted at. "So, what do we do first? We don't have the tools or the space, and we're still stuck here with our foster parents."

"We start by focusing on what we can control," Suzie said, her voice steady. "Claus mentioned the workshop. We need to find out more about it, see if we can access it, and start planning from there."

Sandy nodded, feeling a surge of determination. "Right. And we'll have to be careful. We can't let our foster parents get suspicious. We'll need to be smart about this."

As they discussed their next steps, the feeling of uncertainty began to lift, replaced by a sense of purpose. They knew their journey would be fraught with challenges, but the presence of the notebook and the promise of Claus's support provided a beacon of hope.

In the days that followed, Sandy and Suzie took careful steps to investigate their father's workshop. They managed to obtain the address from Claus's cryptic directions and found themselves standing in front of a weathered building that had seen better days. The workshop was tucked away in a quiet corner of town, its once vibrant paint now chipped and faded. It was as if it had been waiting for them to return.

With a mix of excitement and trepidation, they unlocked the door and stepped inside. The space was dusty and filled with old tools, broken toys, and shelves lined with jars of screws and nails. It was as if their father had left everything exactly as it was before he passed away. The smell of aged wood and metal was comforting, a reminder of the days they had spent together in this very room.

They began to clean and organize the workshop, rediscovering tools and materials that had been untouched for years. The process was both nostalgic and invigorating. Each item they found seemed to carry a piece of their father's spirit, urging them to continue his work.

Meanwhile, they also began researching and planning how to repair toys and furniture. Suzie spent hours reading through books and manuals, while Sandy practiced using the tools they had found. They contacted local suppliers for materials and started gathering information on how to set up their small business. The process was slow, but every small step they took made the dream of carrying on their father's legacy more tangible.

Despite their progress, the shadow of their foster parents' dangerous activities loomed over them. They remained vigilant, knowing that the risks involved were far from over. Sandy and Suzie had to navigate their double lives carefully, maintaining their façade of obedient foster children while working secretly to build their future.

One evening, as they worked late into the night, Suzie looked up from her task and glanced at Sandy. "Do you think Claus will come back? Or is this it?"

Sandy shrugged, a faint smile on his lips. "I think he'll be around, in one way or another. He's got his own way of showing up when we need him. For now, we've got to trust that he's got things under control with our foster parents."

The twins continued their preparations with renewed energy. Their father's legacy was not just a burden but a gift—one that offered them a chance to heal, to make a difference, and to find meaning in their lives once more. Each day brought new challenges, but they faced them with a sense of purpose, driven by the memory of their father and the guidance of a peculiar but kind-hearted detective.

As the holiday season approached, the twins felt a growing anticipation. They knew their journey was just beginning, but they were no longer the lost children who had endured hardship alone. With each repair they completed, each toy they restored, and each piece of their father's legacy they honored, they were building something new—something filled with hope, purpose, and the promise of a brighter future.

Chapter 6

A Curious Discovery

The weekend arrived, and the twins, Sandy and Suzie, found themselves alone as their foster parents went off on one of their frequent "secret" ventures. David and Leigh Boyce, their foster parents, ran a business specializing in high-end security systems. Their partners, Patty and Garry Panton, had a complementary business installing these systems. Both couples often collaborated, traveling extensively through New York State and Massachusetts, with their primary client base centered in Albany. This constant traveling and their mysterious absences had long aroused the twins' curiosity, but it was only during this particular weekend that they decided to investigate further.

Suzie, ever the perceptive one, was standing near David while he took a phone call from Patty. Suzie positioned herself strategically, hoping to overhear something that might shed light on their foster parents' secretive activities. The conversation unfolded in a way that would forever change the twins' understanding of their foster parents.

"Hello Patty," David greeted, his voice slightly muffled as he answered the call. The phone was on speaker mode, allowing Suzie to hear both sides of the conversation.

"Hi David," Patty responded. "Are we all set for the weekend?"

David's voice was tinged with excitement. "We sure are. This will be our best job yet. We've already lined up buyers for the really expensive items and some of the artwork. We're set to leave Friday night and will be back Sunday evening. We have an early meeting with the lawyers on Sunday morning."

The mention of lawyers piqued Suzie's interest. She listened intently as David continued. "Can we trust the lawyers?"

"Yes, we've worked with them before," Patty assured him. "They've been very helpful with handling the products."

David's next words sent a chill down Suzie's spine. "This is going to be our first million-dollar job. Leigh and I are excited but also a bit nervous."

Patty echoed the sentiment. "We're excited too. Let's meet up tomorrow when the kids are at school."

"Sure thing," David replied. "See you at 10:00 AM at your place."

The call ended, and David walked out of the room, leaving Suzie stunned. It sounded as though their foster parents were involved in something illegal, and the fact that they were excited about a "million-dollar job" only fueled her suspicion. Suzie's heart raced as she rushed to find her twin brother, Sandy.

When the siblings reunited, Suzie shared the details of what she had overheard. Sandy listened carefully, his expression turning serious. "If what you heard is true, it sounds like they're planning something criminal," Sandy said thoughtfully.

"We need to be careful," Suzie said. "We shouldn't confront them yet. Let's observe and see if we can find more evidence before doing anything."

The twins decided to keep their discovery to themselves, opting to observe their foster parents' activities closely. They continued their routine, attending school and living their daily lives, all while secretly monitoring their foster parents' movements.

The week passed with the twins shadowing their foster parents as they visited various locations. They noted the addresses and times of their trips but remained unsure about their next steps. The twins knew their foster parents cared for them, but they were also wary of how the revelation might affect their relationship with them.

After their father's death, Sandy and Suzie had been forced into foster care. The sudden shift from running their family toy business to adapting to their new lives had been jarring. The twins had tried to continue the toy business part-time after school, but the demands of their foster care situation made it impractical. They eventually had to close down the factory and shut up shop, an emotional decision that left them feeling disconnected from their past.

The knowledge of their foster parents' potentially criminal activities ignited a spark within the twins. They began to entertain the idea of becoming burglars themselves, but without connections to sell their stolen goods, they decided to follow a Robin Hood-like approach. Their plan was to steal from the wealthy and distribute their finds to those in need.

Their first attempt at burglary was cautiously planned. They targeted a pair of high-end bicycles, which they left outside a home they believed belonged to a family with six children who could benefit from the "gift." The twins were exhilarated by their initial success, not fully grasping the gravity of their actions or the fact that what they were doing was illegal.

The twins' second foray into burglary was more ambitious. They aimed to steal expensive mountain bikes from a large house rumored to be owned by a wealthy family involved in drug dealing. The plan was meticulously crafted to coincide with their foster parents' activities to avoid arousing suspicion.

On the night of the burglary, the twins approached the target house, their hearts pounding with anticipation. They found the house shrouded in darkness, with all lights turned off. The cloudy sky added to the sense of secrecy and danger. Using their headlights, they managed to locate and begin wheeling the mountain bikes away from the house.

Suddenly, their excitement turned to terror. The blaring sound of fire alarms pierced the night, and spotlights illuminated the property, bathing it in harsh, glaring light. The twins were startled as sirens wailed in the distance, growing louder with each passing second. The arrival of police officers was imminent.

Panicking, Sandy and Suzie abandoned the bikes, their earlier bravado replaced by sheer fright. They stood frozen, their breath coming in ragged gasps as the police closed in. Their brief stint as burglars ended abruptly, their aspirations of becoming master thieves shattered.

The police arrived swiftly, their patrol cars flashing with red and blue lights. Officers approached the twins, their stern expressions reflecting the seriousness of the situation. Sandy and Suzie were escorted to the police station, their hearts heavy with the weight of their predicament.

At the station, the twins were questioned about their actions. The officers were stern but fair, their questions probing the reasons behind the twins' desperate actions. Sandy and Suzie explained their motives, their voices trembling as they recounted their experiences and the suspicions that led them to act.

The police, though sympathetic to their plight, had to follow protocol. They informed the twins that their actions constituted a crime, and they would need to face the consequences. However, considering their age and the circumstances that led to their actions, the officers decided not to press serious charges. Instead, they would be placed under the supervision of a trusted figure who could guide them and address the issues that had led to their criminal behavior.

As they awaited further instructions, Sandy and Suzie reflected on their choices and the lessons they had learned. Their journey into the world of crime had been short-lived, but it had exposed them to the harsh realities of their situation and the need for a better path forward.

Chapter 7
A New Path Forward

The twins, Sandy and Suzie, were escorted to the Grahamsville police station, their hearts heavy with apprehension. They were met by a short, round man with a lush white beard, his presence somehow both comforting and intimidating. "All right, Sarge," he said with a confident nod, "I'll take it from here."

"Hello, Denise and Ken," he began, his voice warm and reassuring. "My name is Detective Sherlock Claus, and I've been watching you for quite some time—many years, in fact."

The twins, still trembling from their recent ordeal, sat quietly, their nerves frayed and their eyes downcast.

"You've been dealt a tough hand and have coped remarkably well under the circumstances," Detective Claus continued. "I'm truly sorry for the loss you've endured. Losing those who were so close to you is never easy."

Detective Claus's words carried a weight of empathy and understanding. He was known for his experience and had a reputation for being both firm and fair. "I am aware of your recent actions, both tonight and a few weeks ago. While your intentions were good, the actions themselves were not. Fortunately, the situation is not as dire as it might seem."

The twins exchanged puzzled glances. Claus continued, "The skates and bikes you took were replaced almost immediately—within hours for the skates and within five minutes for the bikes. The homeowners whose property you visited tonight were not at home, and everything has been restored to its original state."

The twins' relief was palpable, though they remained apprehensive.

"Even though what you did was wrong, there will be no further action taken. Incidentally, the house you visited tonight belongs to a wealthy family who are honest, hardworking individuals, not the criminals you suspected."

Detective Claus paused for a moment, allowing his words to sink in. "I have a proposition for you. I would like you to consider using the skills your father taught you. Would you be interested in mending broken toys, just as he did?"

The twins' faces lit up with a mixture of hope and excitement. They had long admired their father's ability to repair and restore, and this opportunity seemed like a beacon of light in their dark times.

"I knew your dad," Claus said, his voice softer. "Not very well, but we did some business together."

"Yes!!" Sandy and Suzie exclaimed in unison, their voices filled with enthusiasm.

"Here's how it will work," Claus explained. "You will need to create some business letterhead and decide on a name for your venture. Design flyers that advertise your services for repairing broken items, just as your father did."

He handed them an envelope. "This is for your startup costs. You should use this money to cover your initial expenses. Remember, this business must be managed outside of school hours. Your education is important, even though it may seem less relevant now. You have the experience from your father to fall back on."

The twins accepted the envelope with gratitude. Claus continued, "You will need to distribute the flyers and personally introduce yourselves to homeowners. Ask them if they have any damaged toys their children would still like."

"Since you're both too young to drive, you'll have to find a way to get the toys back to your father's workshop. This is a challenge you'll need to address," he said with a knowing look.

"If you require additional funds, you can come to the police station and ask the duty officers for another envelope. It will be found under the in-tray with your names on it. No questions will be asked, and you can use the money however you need."

"Any toys you receive must be repaired and ready for collection within two weeks. You should not take on more than you can handle," Claus warned.

He added, "Your foster parents will be informed about your new commitment, and they will understand that you need time outside school hours. If things become too difficult, you can quit at any time and keep any remaining funds."

Detective Claus stood up, signaling that his time was up. "If you need to contact me, call this number, and I will get back to you."

With that, Claus left the room. The twins noticed that he did not speak to anyone else as he exited the police station. His presence had been almost ghostly, and they were left bewildered by his departure.

Moments later, the officer in charge entered and told them they were free to go. "You're not needed here any longer. The entire night can be forgotten," he said.

As they stepped outside the police station, the twins looked at each other in confusion. "What just happened?" they asked simultaneously. It was 3:00 a.m., and they were anxious about their late return home. They knew their foster parents would likely notice their absence if they arrived too early.

Finding their home empty, the twins decided to meet the next day. Living so close to each other was a blessing, and they agreed to reconvene on Sunday.

The excitement of the previous night made sleep elusive. When they met the following day, they had much to discuss. The first topic was Detective Sherlock Claus and his peculiar visit. They wondered why the other police officers seemed unaware of his presence.

Two things were clear: they wanted to build a business they could be proud of, and they were determined to avoid a life of crime. Their brief experience as burglars had been enough to convince them that this was not the path they wished to follow.

They needed a memorable name for their business and effective flyers to advertise their services. After much deliberation, they settled on a name and designed their flyers. They also decided on distinctive uniforms in green and red.

Fortunately, the manager of the local print shop agreed to produce their flyers for free, allowing them to start their business without any initial costs. The $1,000 given to them by Detective Claus remained untouched.

Unsure of how many customers they would attract, they distributed only forty flyers to the homes nearest to them and to their father's factory, just a mile away. They waited a week before following up on their distribution.

To their surprise, they received twenty-two requests for repairs. They chose to focus on wooden and metal toys, avoiding plastic items except for soft plastic dolls due to environmental concerns. Their choice was well-received by their customers.

Like their father, Sandy and Suzie only requested payment to cover material costs. However, their craftsmanship led many customers to "slip them a dollar or two" when picking up their beautifully repaired toys. Their savings began to accumulate, and they decided to use the money towards buying a pickup truck once they obtained their driver's licenses.

As the final year of school progressed, the twins found themselves increasingly occupied with their new business. Their weekends and after-school hours were consumed by toy repairs. They planned to distribute flyers every two weeks, but the volume of work allowed them to extend the interval to three weeks after the first drop.

Their second round of door knocking, following the flyer distribution, resulted in fifty-three repair jobs from just thirty houses. The twins were astonished by the overwhelming response. Word of their services spread rapidly, and they knew they needed a plan and additional help to manage the growing demand.

Thus, their journey into the world of toy repair and their commitment to honoring their father's legacy had begun, setting them on a path of hard work, community engagement, and personal growth.

Chapter 8

A FAMILY SECRET REVEALED

Denise's eyes widened in shock as she stood frozen in the doorway, having overheard the secret conversation between David and Patty. The weight of the revelation hit her like a physical force, leaving her momentarily paralyzed. She could barely breathe as the gravity of the situation sank in, and her mind struggled to piece together the fragments of what she had just heard. Fear gripped her heart, sending cold shivers down her spine. She was overwhelmed by a tumultuous mix of emotions—confusion, anxiety, and a growing sense of dread.

David, his face a mixture of concern and urgency, noticed Denise standing there. His expression hardened, and he quickly turned to Patty. "Denise heard our conversation," he said, his voice taut with tension. "Bring Garry and come here immediately. And make sure to bring Ken as well, but don't mention why."

Patty's face reflected the same concern, but she quickly nodded and left the room to carry out David's instructions. Her footsteps echoed faintly in the hallway as she went to fetch Garry and Ken. David's stern demeanor contrasted sharply with the usually warm and approachable persona he projected. His eyes, usually kind and reassuring, now held a steely determination.

The foster parents had always worked hard to maintain an image of normalcy and kindness. They prided themselves on creating a nurturing environment for the twins, and their public persona was that of generous, ethical people who ran their own business and helped those in need. Their kindness was genuine and deeply rooted in their character, but it was now overshadowed by the troubling secret they harbored.

As Denise stood alone, the house seemed eerily quiet. The usual sounds of domestic life—laughter, the clinking of dishes, the soft hum of conversation—were replaced by a heavy silence that pressed in on her. Her mind raced with questions. What was this secret they were keeping? How serious was it? And why was it so important to keep Ken and Garry in the dark until now?

Within twenty minutes, the emergency meeting was set. The gathering took place around the large dining table, which had been the center of many family dinners and celebrations. Tonight, however, it was the setting for an uncharacteristically somber and tense meeting. The atmosphere was heavy with unease, and the usual warmth of the room seemed to have been replaced by a chilling apprehension.

David, Patty, Garry, and Leigh sat at one end of the table, their expressions grim. The adults kept the twins apart, speaking in hushed tones as they deliberated their next course of action. The room was filled with an oppressive silence, punctuated only by the occasional rustle of papers or the soft clinking of a coffee cup being set down.

Denise sat with her back straight and her hands clenched tightly in her lap. Her mind was a whirlwind of anxiety and confusion. The image of David and Patty, who had always seemed so dependable and caring, was now marred by the secret they were hiding. Her heart pounded in her chest, and she could feel the knot tightening in her stomach. The weight of the impending revelation felt almost unbearable.

Ken and Garry arrived shortly after Patty, their faces reflecting a mix of curiosity and concern. Ken, who was usually calm and collected, looked noticeably troubled. Garry, ever the supportive presence, gave Denise a reassuring nod, but his own anxiety was evident in the furrow of his brow.

Once everyone was seated, David cleared his throat and began to speak. His voice, though steady, carried an undertone of seriousness. "Thank you all for coming on such short notice. I'm afraid we have some difficult matters to discuss."

Patty, sitting beside him, nodded in agreement. "We need to explain something important that affects all of us. It's not easy to share this, but we believe it's necessary for you to understand."

Denise's heart sank as she listened. David and Patty's criminal activities were about to be laid bare. The words felt like a punch to the gut, and she struggled to keep her composure as David continued.

"We've been involved in activities that are not legal," David said slowly, choosing his words with care. "Our actions might seem severe, but we want to assure you that we never intended to harm anyone. Our victims are wealthy, and we tried to minimize the impact on their lives."

Denise's mind reeled as she tried to process this new information. The notion that the people she had trusted and admired were involved in criminal behavior was almost too much to bear. She looked at Ken, whose face was a mask of shock and disbelief.

Leigh, who had been silent until now, spoke up. "We know this is a lot to take in. We're not asking for your approval, but we want you to understand the context and the reasons behind our decisions."

The conversation that followed was filled with tense exchanges and emotional outbursts. Denise's struggle to maintain her composure became increasingly difficult as she tried to grasp the full extent of what was being revealed. She was overwhelmed by a flood of questions and doubts, but the adults' serious demeanor left little room for interruption.

The meeting continued late into the evening, with each person grappling with the shocking revelations in their own way. Denise's mind was a whirlwind of thoughts, and she found it hard to focus on any single aspect of the conversation. The knot in her stomach remained, a constant reminder of the uncertainty and fear that now hung over her.

As the meeting drew to a close, Denise knew that the road ahead would be challenging. The secrets that had been uncovered were bound to have lasting repercussions, and she was left to navigate the uncertain future with the weight of the truth now firmly in her hands.

Ken, on the other hand, was bewildered. He sat in his chair, his mind racing with a storm of thoughts. What could have triggered this sudden, secretive meeting? His heart pounded in his chest as he tried to piece together the puzzle. Had they done something wrong? Was there an issue with the foster arrangement? The uncertainty gnawed at him, making his stomach churn.

Garry, noticing the distress on Denise's face, turned to her with a soft, reassuring tone. "Denise, could you please tell us exactly what you heard? We need to make sure we're clear on this before we proceed."

Denise's hands trembled as she clutched her sweater tightly. Her voice was barely above a whisper as she spoke, "I overheard something about you planning to rob a house and then sell the stolen items. I'm so confused right now. Why are you telling Ken and me this? What's going on?"

Patty, sitting beside Garry, looked at Denise with a resigned expression. Her shoulders slumped slightly, and she sighed before speaking. "Yes, Denise, I'm afraid what you heard is accurate. We do engage in criminal activities. It's not something we're proud of, but it is the truth."

Ken's face fell as he absorbed the weight of Patty's words. He felt a cold shock run through him. "But you've always treated us like family," he said, his voice filled with disbelief. "I never imagined that you could be involved in something like this. It just doesn't make sense."

The room fell into a heavy silence as the gravity of the situation settled over them. Ken's words hung in the air, a stark contrast to the image of the caring, supportive foster parents he had known for so long. The silence was punctuated only by the quiet hum of the old radiator in the corner, which seemed almost mocking in its calmness.

Patty finally broke the silence with a weary sigh. "I'm sorry to disappoint you, Ken," she said softly. "But Denise's understanding is correct. We've chosen a path that we believe is justified, in our own way. We see ourselves as modern-day Robin Hoods. Our security business gives us access to many homes, often those of the wealthy. We target those homes to redistribute the wealth we acquire, or so we tell ourselves."

Garry nodded in agreement. "It's not something we take lightly," he added, his voice more serious now. "We've been doing this for years, and while we might not always follow the law, we do have our own code. We target those who we believe can afford to lose a bit. But I understand if this is difficult for you to hear. It was never our intention to deceive you."

Ken looked between Garry and Patty, his mind struggling to process the new reality. "But why didn't you ever tell us before? Why hide it if it's a part of who you are?"

Patty looked down at her hands, her fingers intertwined nervously. "We've tried to shield you from this side of our lives. We thought it was better for you not to know, to protect you from the moral conflict we face. We didn't want to taint the trust we've built with you."

Denise's gaze was steady, though her voice remained faint. "I wish I had known sooner. It would have helped me understand why things always seemed so contradictory."

Garry's expression softened as he looked at Denise. "We never meant to cause you distress. This is a lot to take in, and we understand if you need time to process it all."

Ken swallowed hard, trying to gather his thoughts. "I need some time too," he said finally. "This is a lot to digest, and I need to figure out where this leaves us."

The room was heavy with the weight of unspoken words and unresolved feelings. Each person sat in their own private turmoil, struggling to reconcile the past with the new reality that had just been revealed.

Garry leaned forward, a look of conviction on his face as he said, "We use our extensive knowledge of security systems to identify and target homes where the owners are either corrupt or actively engaged in criminal activities themselves. Our philosophy is to take from those whom we deem to be morally questionable. It's about redistributing wealth from those who exploit their positions for wrongdoing."

Denise, her brow furrowing in concern, interjected, "But why do you do this? Is there violence involved? And more importantly, why are you telling us all of this now?"

Patty, who had been listening intently, took a deep breath before responding. "We've been operating this way for about five or six years now. Over that time, we've honed our skills and refined our methods. A significant turning point came when we met someone named Mr. Adrian Claus. He was a mysterious figure, well-versed in our activities, and approached us with an intriguing offer. He proposed to assist us in our operations, suggesting ways to streamline our efforts and navigate our criminal activities more effectively."

Ken's expression was a mixture of curiosity and bewilderment. "I don't understand. Why bring Adrian Claus into this? What's his role?"

David, who had been silent until now, chose this moment to speak. "Let me explain. Seven years ago, I was hired to provide a quote for installing a security system for a client. While I was preparing for the presentation, I happened to notice a valuable antique cabinet being unloaded from a truck. It caught my eye because it was unmistakably the same piece that had been stolen from a local church not long before. Garry and I discussed the situation and decided we should report it. However, before we could act, Adrian Claus approached us. He proposed a partnership where we would work together to return the cabinet without becoming directly involved in the potentially dangerous aftermath."

Denise's eyes widened as she absorbed the gravity of David's words. "So, this Adrian Claus, he's been involved with you for a long time?"

David nodded. "Yes, he has. His involvement has been crucial. Claus has a network and connections that have helped us immensely. His expertise and resources have allowed us to return stolen items discreetly and with minimal risk. While our initial intention was to do the right thing by returning the cabinet, Claus offered us a way to continue our operations without directly compromising our safety."

Patty added, "Claus has been a significant figure in our lives, providing not just advice but also logistical support. He's introduced us to methods that have made our operations more efficient and less risky. His connections have also helped us avoid legal troubles that could have jeopardized everything we've worked for."

Ken, still processing the information, asked, "So, what happens now? What's your plan moving forward?"

Garry looked at the group, his gaze steady and resolute. "Our plan is to keep refining our methods and using the expertise we've gained over the years. We continue to target those we believe are morally corrupt, with the understanding that we're operating in a complex and often dangerous world. Our goal is to stay ahead of any potential threats and ensure that our operations remain as secure and effective as possible."

Denise's expression softened slightly, but she still looked concerned. "It sounds like you're all deeply involved in something that's more complex than I initially realized. How do you manage the risks associated with this?"

Patty replied, "We're very careful about how we operate. We have protocols in place to ensure our safety and to minimize the risk of getting caught. We've also developed a network of trusted contacts who help us manage various aspects of our operations."

As the group continued their discussion, the weight of the revelations hung in the air, each member grappling with the implications of their choices and the future that lay ahead. The complexity of their situation was clear, and the road forward was fraught with challenges, but they remained united in their resolve to navigate their path with caution and determination.

"Adrian Claus, a well-known figure in certain circles, offered us guidance and support. He revealed that the homeowner, Mr. Crooks, was a career criminal who dealt in stolen antiques and gold bullion. Initially, we were reluctant to accept his help, but Claus's deep knowledge and his offer of assistance drew us into a more complex world of crime than we had ever imagined."

Denise and Ken sat in stunned silence, trying to process the enormity of what they had just heard. The world they had known, with its seemingly normal routines and comforting familiarity, was now an elaborate facade that had been carefully constructed by their foster parents. The revelation that their foster father, Mr. Crooks, was deeply entangled in criminal activities, dealing in stolen antiques and gold bullion, was a blow to their sense of security.

Ken, his face pale and eyes wide with disbelief, finally broke the silence. "Isn't there any other way to live? Why resort to crime?" His voice was a mixture of anguish and confusion.

David's shoulders sagged as he looked at the twins with a mixture of regret and sorrow. "We've found ourselves entangled in this web of deceit and crime, believing it was a means to an end. We never set out to hurt anyone. We thought we were making the best decisions for survival and success, but now we see that our actions have led to consequences we hadn't fully anticipated."

Patty, who had been quiet until now, added with a tone of deep remorse, "We wanted to explain this to you, hoping you'd understand the complexities of our situation. We've always tried to care for you as best as we could, despite our flaws. It was never our intention to deceive or harm you. We thought we were protecting you from the harsh realities of our world, but now we realize that we've only made things worse."

Denise's eyes were filled with tears as she struggled to reconcile the image of the loving, supportive guardians she had known with the reality of their criminal undertakings. "But how could you hide this from us? How could you live such a double life?"

Patty's voice trembled as she tried to explain. "It wasn't easy for us, Denise. We were trying to shield you from the dangers of our world, and in doing so, we lost sight of how our actions would impact you. We were trying to protect you by keeping you in the dark, but now we see that our secrecy has only led to more pain and confusion."

David looked at the twins with a pained expression, his own sense of failure evident. "We never wanted to deceive you. We hoped that by guiding you through this complex world, we could help you navigate it safely. But we understand now that we've only contributed to your distress."

As the meeting continued, the air was thick with a mixture of explanations and justifications. Denise and Ken listened, their hearts heavy with the weight of betrayal and disillusionment. The foster parents, who had once been their pillars of strength and guidance, were now revealed to be deeply flawed individuals living in a shadowy world of crime.

The conversation gradually came to a close, leaving Denise and Ken to grapple with the revelations they had just received. The future stretched out before them, shrouded in uncertainty and the lingering sting of betrayal. They faced the daunting task of reconciling their love and respect for their foster parents with the harsh reality of their criminal activities.

As the meeting ended, Denise and Ken were left alone with their thoughts. The familiar world they had known had been irrevocably altered, and they faced an uncertain future, struggling to come to terms with the betrayal of those they had trusted most. The road ahead was fraught with challenges, but one truth was undeniable: their lives would never be the same again.

Chapter 9

A New Journey Begins

The air outside the police station was crisp, carrying the light fragrance of blooming flowers from the nearby park. Sandy and Suzie, the twin sisters, stood side by side on the steps of the station, their hearts racing with a mixture of anxiety and hope. The wait had been long and trying, filled with restless nights and countless thoughts about their uncertain future. Each day had seemed like an endless loop of waiting and wondering, but today was different. Today, they hoped for some clarity.

They had been pondering their next steps for weeks now, unsure of what lay ahead and feeling a growing sense of urgency. Detective Claus, who had been a steady figure of support throughout their ordeal, was the person they had come to rely on for guidance. His presence had been a source of comfort, and they trusted him to provide the answers they desperately needed.

As they stood there, glancing at their watches and then at each other, the minutes seemed to stretch out endlessly. Just when it felt like they might lose hope, Detective Claus appeared from around the corner. His tall, composed figure emerged against the backdrop of the bright sky, cutting a calm and reassuring silhouette. The sight of him immediately brought a sense of relief to the twins, their faces lighting up with a mix of anticipation and gratitude.

"Hello, Detective Claus," Sandy greeted him warmly, her voice carrying a blend of nervous excitement and relief. She could hardly keep the tremor out of her voice as she spoke.

"Hello, Sandy and Suzie. It's good to see you both," Detective Claus responded with a gentle smile. His voice, deep and measured, was filled with a warmth that soothed their frayed nerves. "Shall we head over to the park across the street? It's a beautiful day, and I thought it might be more comfortable to talk there."

The twins exchanged a look of relief and nodded eagerly. The park, with its serene landscape and vibrant greenery, promised a welcome contrast to the sterile and impersonal environment of the police station. The thought of sitting on a park bench and discussing their future amidst the tranquility of nature was far more appealing.

They followed Detective Claus as he led the way, their footsteps in sync as they crossed the street. The cool breeze played gently with their hair, and the scent of fresh blossoms lingered in the air, enhancing the feeling of calm. The park was just a short walk away, but the transition from the harsh reality of the police station to the peaceful park was almost palpable.

Upon arriving at the park, they found a quiet bench beneath a large oak tree, its branches swaying slightly in the gentle breeze. The sunlight filtered through the leaves, casting dappled shadows on the ground. Detective Claus gestured for them to sit, and the twins settled onto the bench, their posture a mix of eagerness and apprehension.

"So, what's been on your minds lately?" Detective Claus asked, taking a seat beside them. His tone was casual yet attentive, as if he were genuinely interested in understanding their thoughts and concerns.

Sandy took a deep breath before speaking. "We've been trying to figure out what comes next for us. It's been so overwhelming, and we just don't know where to turn."

Suzie nodded in agreement, her expression one of quiet determination. "We're ready to move forward, but we need some guidance on what steps to take. It's hard not knowing what our future holds."

Detective Claus listened intently, his gaze thoughtful. "I understand. It's a challenging situation, but I'm here to help you navigate through it. I've been working on finding a solution that ensures you both have the support and stability you need."

The twins felt a glimmer of hope as they listened. Detective Claus had always been a steady source of support, and his words carried the promise of a solution. The park's serene surroundings seemed to amplify the sense of possibility that was beginning to take root in their hearts.

After a brief pause, Detective Claus continued, "I've been in touch with some local agencies and resources that specialize in helping families in transition. They can offer support and guidance tailored to your specific needs. Additionally, there are some options for temporary housing and counseling services that I believe would be beneficial for you."

Sandy and Suzie exchanged a look of relief, the tension in their shoulders visibly easing. The prospect of having a plan and knowing that there were resources available to help them navigate this difficult period was a significant comfort.

"Thank you, Detective Claus," Suzie said, her voice tinged with gratitude. "We really appreciate everything you've done for us."

Detective Claus nodded, his smile reflecting genuine warmth. "It's my pleasure. I want to make sure that you both have the support you need to move forward. You've shown incredible strength, and I believe that with the right resources, you'll be able to build a positive future for yourselves."

As the conversation continued, the twins felt a renewed sense of optimism. The park, with its peaceful ambiance and the gentle rustling of leaves, provided a perfect backdrop for their discussion. They talked about their options, the resources available to them, and the steps they needed to take. Each word from Detective Claus was like a stepping stone, guiding them toward a clearer path.

The sun began to dip lower in the sky, casting a golden hue over the park. The twins, now feeling more at ease, appreciated the time and care Detective Claus had taken to explain everything in detail. The sense of uncertainty that had weighed heavily on them seemed to lift, replaced by a growing confidence that they were moving in the right direction.

As they stood to leave, Detective Claus gave them a reassuring nod. "If you have any more questions or need further assistance, don't hesitate to reach out. I'll be here to support you every step of the way."

Sandy and Suzie thanked him once again, their hearts lighter than when they had arrived. As they walked back toward the police station, the park's tranquil beauty seemed to reflect their newfound hope. The future, once shrouded in uncertainty, now appeared a bit clearer, thanks to the guidance and support of Detective Claus.

Once seated on a park bench under the shade of an old oak tree, Detective Claus leaned back, a contemplative expression on his face. The park was quiet, save for the occasional rustle of leaves in the gentle breeze. The dappled sunlight filtered through the branches, casting a warm, speckled glow on the ground. Claus took a deep breath, enjoying the peaceful surroundings before turning his attention to the twins.

"You know," he began, his tone thoughtful, "your seventeenth birthday is next week. It's the perfect time to start thinking about getting your driver's licenses. Have either of you thought about taking the driving tests?"

Sandy and Suzie exchanged uncertain glances. For a moment, they were silent, contemplating the idea. The notion of driving had always seemed like a distant dream, something to think about only in the far-off future. It wasn't that they hadn't thought about it; they had. But with their current situation, it felt like a luxury rather than a necessity. They had more immediate concerns—like figuring out how they were going to manage day-to-day expenses, let alone afford a car.

"I mean," Suzie started hesitantly, her voice tinged with doubt, "we've thought about it. But we're really not sure if it's something we can afford right now. Money is so tight, and driving seems like it's... well, a bit beyond us at the moment."

Detective Claus, always keenly perceptive, appeared to have anticipated their concern. He regarded them with a kind, understanding gaze. "I understand that money is a bit tight for you both," he said gently, his voice steady and reassuring. "But I want you to know that you've worked incredibly hard. You've earned more than you might realize.

The funds you've saved up, along with what I left for you after our last meeting, should be more than enough to get you started."

The twins' eyes widened in surprise. The idea of having enough to not only take the driving tests but to also purchase a car seemed almost surreal. They exchanged another glance, their initial shock turning into a mix of hope and disbelief.

"Wait, you really think we can afford to buy a car?" Sandy asked, her voice a mix of astonishment and cautious optimism. Her heart raced slightly at the prospect, but she was still trying to grasp the reality of what Claus was suggesting.

Detective Claus nodded with confidence. "Absolutely. You've earned it. And I'll even help you find a good deal on a vehicle. There are plenty of affordable pickup trucks for sale. I'll make sure you get one that's not only reliable but also fits within your budget. Once you've passed your driving tests, I'll have it registered in both your names. You won't have to worry about a thing."

Sandy and Suzie's faces lit up with a blend of relief and excitement. The prospect of having their own vehicle, and the independence that came with it, was a bright spot in their lives. They could already imagine how different things might be, how much easier it would be to manage their daily routines and responsibilities.

"You really don't have to do this," Suzie said, her voice filled with gratitude. "We're grateful for everything you've already done for us."

Detective Claus smiled warmly, his eyes twinkling with kindness. "It's my pleasure. You both deserve a break, and I know how important this is for you. Think of it as a step toward the future. A small reward for all your hard work and perseverance."

As they continued to talk, the conversation shifted to practicalities—the driving test schedules, the types of vehicles that might be suitable for their needs, and the steps they needed to take to get everything in order. Claus offered to accompany them to the driving school and help with the paperwork involved in purchasing a car. His support was more than just financial; it was a gesture of genuine care and encouragement.

The afternoon wore on, the park remaining a tranquil haven as they discussed their plans. The initial anxiety and apprehension the twins had felt began to fade, replaced by a sense of hope and determination. With Detective Claus's support, they could envision a future where they had the means to drive, manage their daily tasks more effectively, and gain a newfound sense of independence.

As they prepared to leave, Sandy and Suzie thanked Claus once more, their voices filled with sincerity and appreciation. The oak tree's leaves rustled gently, and the park seemed to echo with a renewed sense of possibility for the twins. With a final handshake and warm goodbyes, they parted ways, their hearts lighter and their minds buzzing with the exciting new chapter that lay ahead.

The excitement that had been bubbling beneath the surface suddenly burst forth like a burst of sunlight breaking through the clouds. Suzie, still trying to process the whirlwind of emotions and information she had just received, turned to her twin sister with a furrowed brow. "But what if we fail our tests?" she asked, her voice tinged with worry. "What happens then?"

Detective Claus, who had been quietly observing their reactions, let out a gentle chuckle. His demeanor remained as calm and composed as ever, a reassuring anchor amidst their sea of uncertainty. "You're not going to fail," he said, his voice steady and comforting. "You've got this. Just focus on the road and stay calm. I have full confidence in both of you."

The twins exchanged glances, the weight of doubt slowly lifting from their shoulders. Detective Claus had always been a pillar of support for them, his belief in their abilities unwavering even when they struggled with their own self-doubt. His confidence was like a beacon, guiding them through the fog of their insecurities and making them feel as though they could tackle any challenge that came their way.

"You know," Detective Claus continued, a warm smile spreading across his face, "I've seen a lot of people come and go, but you two, you've got something special. You approach everything with such determination and heart. That's why I'm sure you'll do just fine."

Suzie's eyes brightened a bit, and a small smile began to form on her lips. Her sister, Sandy, nodded in agreement, feeling the same surge of renewed confidence. It was remarkable how a few words of encouragement could shift their perspective and refocus their energies.

"We'll meet here again in one week," Detective Claus said as he stood up from the bench, his movements deliberate and measured. "Same time, 3:00 PM. By then, you'll have passed your tests. I'll be here to discuss the next steps with you."

The twins watched intently as Detective Claus began to walk away, his steps purposeful and steady. As he moved further down the path, the twins were left with a renewed sense of excitement and anticipation. It wasn't just about the driving test anymore. The stakes felt higher, and the future seemed to open up before them like an endless horizon.

Sandy turned to Suzie, her eyes gleaming with enthusiasm. "Can you believe it? It feels like everything is finally falling into place. Like we're really moving forward."

Suzie nodded, her earlier anxiety replaced by a sense of determination. "Yeah, it's like we're on the verge of something big. I'm excited, but I'm also really grateful for Detective Claus' support. It makes such a difference knowing that someone believes in us."

They took a deep breath, their spirits lifted by the detective's words. It was clear that this moment was more than just a checkpoint in their journey; it was a significant step toward their future, a future that now seemed full of possibilities. The thought of reuniting with Detective Claus in a week's time to discuss their progress was both thrilling and reassuring.

As they walked away from the bench, their footsteps were lighter, and their conversation was filled with hopeful plans and dreams. They talked about their preparations for the test, sharing ideas and strategies to ensure they would be ready. Each word exchanged was infused with a new sense of purpose and optimism.

The world seemed to expand with every step they took, and they felt as though they were finally stepping into a larger, more exciting chapter of their lives. The challenges ahead seemed manageable with their newfound confidence, and the future, once shrouded in uncertainty, now sparkled with the promise of new opportunities and adventures.

By the time they reached their destination, the twins were practically buzzing with excitement. They knew that their journey was far from over, but they were eager to embrace whatever lay ahead, buoyed by the support and encouragement they had received.

The driving test was no longer just a hurdle to overcome; it had become a gateway to their dreams and aspirations. And as they prepared to face this challenge, they did so with a renewed sense of determination, ready to make the most of the opportunities that awaited them.

The following week seemed to fly by, and before Sandy and Suzie could fully grasp it, the day of their driving tests had arrived. They stood outside the testing center, their hands tightly gripping their driving manuals as they anxiously reviewed last-minute instructions. The sky above was clear, but the weight of the moment was heavy on their shoulders. Their nerves were taut, like a bowstring ready to snap. They hadn't practiced nearly as much as they had planned, and now, the reality of their preparation—or lack thereof—was sinking in.

Sandy, always the more cautious and reserved of the two, was the first to face the challenge. As she approached the car with her name on the test schedule, she took a deep breath, trying to steady her racing heart. The examiner, Christopher Claus, stood by the car, his demeanor calm and reassuring. Christopher was a relative of Detective Claus, a connection that didn't escape Sandy's notice. She wondered if he was aware of the pressure she was feeling, but his friendly nod seemed to offer some comfort.

"Good luck, Sandy," he said, his voice warm. "Just remember to stay calm and follow the instructions."

Sandy nodded, her throat tight with nerves. She took her seat in the driver's seat, her fingers gripping the steering wheel with a white-knuckled grip. She adjusted the mirrors and took a moment to gather her thoughts. The test began smoothly enough. She navigated the streets with care, obeying the traffic signals, checking her mirrors frequently, and maintaining a steady, controlled speed.

However, as she approached a red light, an unexpected jolt threw both her and Christopher forward. The sudden impact of another car rear-ending them caused Sandy's heart to leap into her throat. The collision wasn't severe, but it was enough to make her hands tremble and her confidence waver. The suddenness of the impact left her disoriented, and she could feel her pulse pounding in her ears.

Christopher's calm voice cut through her panic. "Are you alright, Sandy?" he asked, his tone steady but concerned. He quickly assessed the situation, checking for any visible damage to the vehicle and making sure there were no serious injuries. Sandy managed a shaky nod, her breath coming in uneven gasps.

After a brief moment to ensure everything was okay, Christopher signaled that they could continue with the test. Sandy took another deep breath and tried to steady her nerves. The impact had rattled her, but she focused on the road ahead, determined to finish what she had started. She completed the rest of the test with as much composure as she could muster, but the incident had undoubtedly left its mark. She wasn't sure how well she had performed, but at least the ordeal was over.

As Sandy finished her test, she watched Suzie approach the testing center with a mix of apprehension and hope. Suzie's test was scheduled to follow shortly after Sandy's. Suzie, who had been trying to stay positive despite her own nerves, climbed into the car with a determined look. She had seen her sister's test end with an unexpected twist and hoped that her own experience would be less eventful.

Her test began smoothly. The streets were clear, and Suzie felt a sense of relief as she navigated through the course. She followed the instructions, took turns with confidence, and maintained a steady pace.

Everything seemed to be going according to plan until she reached an intersection.

As Suzie approached a green light, her concentration was interrupted by a vehicle barreling through the red light on the cross street. The car zoomed past with alarming speed, narrowly missing Suzie's own vehicle. The sudden danger sent a jolt of adrenaline through Suzie, and she reacted instinctively. Her foot slammed down on the brake pedal, bringing the car to a sudden, but controlled stop.

The close call left Suzie's heart racing, and she could feel the tension in her shoulders. She glanced over at Christopher, who remained calm and composed, his eyes scanning the road for any further hazards. After a moment, he turned to her with a reassuring nod. "Nice reflexes there, Suzie," he said, a hint of approval in his voice. "Let's continue."

Suzie took a deep breath, trying to calm her racing heart. The rest of the test proceeded without any further incidents. Though the initial shock had unsettled her, she managed to complete the test with as much grace as she could muster under the circumstances. When she finally parked the car and turned off the engine, she felt a mix of relief and exhaustion.

As the two sisters stood outside the testing center, they exchanged looks of mutual understanding and support. The day had been filled with unexpected challenges, but they had faced them together. Their hands gripped their manuals a little less tightly now, and though the outcome was still uncertain, they felt a sense of accomplishment simply in having made it through the tests.

The close call left her heart pounding in her chest, but like her sister, Suzie finished the test with no further issues. When she parked the car at the end of the test, she breathed a sigh of relief, grateful that the near-accident hadn't ended in disaster.

When the twins reunited after their tests, they couldn't help but notice a strange coincidence. Both of their tests had involved near accidents, and in both cases, their examiner, Christopher Claus, had remained unnervingly calm. His demeanor reminded them of Detective Claus—the same unshakable composure in the face of unexpected events.

"It's weird, isn't it?" Suzie remarked as they walked toward the waiting area. "Both of us almost got into accidents, but he didn't even flinch."

Sandy nodded in agreement. "It's like nothing phases him. Just like Detective Claus."

Despite the unsettling incidents, the day ended on a high note. Both twins had passed their driving tests, and the excitement of finally having their licenses overshadowed the earlier scares. They couldn't wait to tell Detective Claus the news.

A week later, the twins returned to the park as planned. Detective Claus was already waiting for them, leaning casually against a lamppost as he watched them approach. There was a glimmer of pride in his eyes as they excitedly told him about their experiences.

"We both passed!" Sandy exclaimed, her face flushed with excitement.

Detective Claus smiled broadly. "I knew you would," he said. "I'm proud of you both. Now, as promised, I've arranged for your vehicle. It's all ready, registered in your names, and waiting for you at the dealership."

The twins could hardly contain their excitement. They were finally getting their own vehicle—a symbol of their newfound independence.

Detective Claus continued, his voice gentle but firm. "Remember, this is just the beginning. There will be more challenges ahead, but you've proven that you can handle whatever comes your way. Take things one step at a time, and don't forget that I'm always here if you need help."

As they stood together in the park, the weight of the past weeks seemed to melt away. The future, once uncertain and intimidating, now seemed filled with possibility. With their licenses in hand and Detective Claus's unwavering support behind them, Sandy and Suzie felt ready to embark on their new journey—one full of hope, challenges, and new beginnings.

Chapter 10

A NEW CHAPTER UNFOLDS

On a crisp Friday afternoon, precisely at 3:00 PM, Sandy and Suzie arrived at the workshop. They were greeted by the sight of Detective Claus, who stood beside an eye-catching new truck. The vehicle was a striking white, adorned with festive green and red stripes that added a cheerful touch. Its large enclosed cage hinted at many upcoming adventures. More than just a mode of transportation, this truck represented the expansion of their business and the beginning of an exciting new chapter in their lives.

As Sandy and Suzie approached the truck, their eyes sparkled with excitement. The possibilities this new truck offered seemed endless. "Can you believe it, Suzie?" Sandy said, her voice brimming with enthusiasm. "We can reach so many more clients now!"

Suzie nodded in agreement, her eyes widening as she inspected the truck. "And with more space, we'll be able to bring in extra help to manage everything. This is going to be amazing!"

Their conversation was interrupted as Detective Claus approached them with a warm smile. "It's wonderful to see you both so excited. This truck is going to be a great asset for your growing business."

Sandy and Suzie thanked him, and as they admired the truck, Detective Claus continued. "I've also got some good news. Your new employee, Elfin Toiz, will be joining you tomorrow. I think you'll find he's a perfect fit for your needs."

The twins recalled how the local newspaper advertisement had quickly brought them the ideal candidate for the job. Elfin Toiz had stumbled upon their ad while enjoying breakfast at his hotel. As he flipped through the employment section, he had noticed the listing under the heading "Experienced Toy Maker Required." The timing was serendipitous; the page had been open right to that section.

Elfin had promptly called them, and Ken, with Denise by his side, had taken the call. Ken had been immediately impressed by Elfin's voice and impressive credentials. Without hesitation, he had offered Elfin the job, asking if he could start the following day. Elfin had accepted the offer with enthusiasm, and it seemed he was exactly what they needed.

The next morning, Sandy and Suzie arrived at the workshop early, eager to meet their new employee. As they walked through the door, their gaze was drawn to a figure waiting by the workbench. Elfin Toiz was dressed in jeans and a vibrant green shirt, adorned with a Christmas tree pattern on the back and holly on the front. The shirt, in particular, highlighted his festive spirit. His beard was neatly trimmed, and his hair, nearly as white as snow, touched the collar of his shirt.

Sandy extended her hand with a friendly smile. "Hi, Elfin! We're so glad to finally meet you."

Elfin shook her hand warmly, his blue eyes twinkling with a friendly glint. "It's great to meet you both as well. I've heard a lot of good things about this place."

Suzie, equally enthusiastic, added, "We're thrilled to have you on board. This truck is just the beginning of a lot of exciting changes for us."

Elfin looked around the workshop with a keen eye. "I can see that. This place has a lot of potential. I'm excited to contribute."

As the twins gave Elfin a tour of the workshop, they discussed their upcoming projects and the new opportunities that the truck would bring. They felt a renewed sense of optimism about their business's future and were eager to get started with Elfin.

The addition of the new truck and Elfin's arrival marked the beginning of an exciting new phase. With their spirits lifted and their team expanded, Sandy and Suzie looked forward to the many adventures that lay ahead.

"Ken and Suzie," Elfin greeted them warmly with a smile, "I'm truly impressed that you've embarked on this venture at such a young age. It's not every day you see young entrepreneurs with such drive and ambition. I see a lot of potential in what you're building here, and I'm genuinely excited to help get it off to a flying start."

Elfin continued with an encouraging tone, "With only a few weeks left before your graduation, I'll take over the factory work for now. This way, you can dedicate your time and energy to your studies and ensure you achieve the grades you deserve. Those high marks might just be crucial for your future endeavors. Just make sure to leave the truck keys with me at the workshop. I'll handle the drive home for you today."

After Elfin had left, Suzie turned to Sandy, her brow furrowed in confusion. "What just happened here? We don't know much about this man, and now we've practically handed him control of everything. Shouldn't we be more cautious?"

Sandy looked thoughtful for a moment before responding. "Yes, we've entrusted him with a lot. But despite that, I don't feel anxious or worried. In fact, I'm oddly at ease. I think we should trust Elfin's expertise and use this time to enjoy our final days of school. It's not every day we get such a chance."

Upon graduating, the twins were both excited and nervous as they returned to the workshop. They were eager to see the progress that Elfin had made. As they stepped inside, they were greeted with an enthusiastic welcome. Elfin met them with a broad grin and led them through the shop.

The transformation was astonishing. The factory was impeccably clean, the floors shining brightly as if freshly polished. The organization was meticulous—everything had its place. New tools and machines were arranged with precision, each set for specific tasks, reflecting a high level of efficiency. The newly added paint room was particularly impressive, fully equipped with state-of-the-art facilities to meet all their needs.

The sight was both overwhelming and exhilarating for the twins. They marveled at how such a compact space could accommodate so many tools and pieces of equipment. Their minds buzzed with questions: Where would new workers come from to handle all the added responsibilities? How would they manage salaries, rent, and the utility bills such as water and electricity?

In addition to the new equipment, there was a large pile of broken toys stacked neatly in one corner. It was a daunting sight, the sheer number suggesting that it might take months to repair them all. However, their eyes were also drawn to a positive aspect of the workshop—there were completed works. Toys that had previously been left for repair were now neatly organized and ready for delivery.

As they took in the full scope of the transformation, the twins couldn't help but feel a mix of awe and relief. The once familiar but cluttered workspace had been transformed into a model of efficiency and order. It was clear that Elfin had invested a great deal of time and effort into the renovation, and his enthusiasm was infectious.

Ken looked at Suzie and said, "This is incredible. I never imagined the workshop could look like this. Elfin really has done a fantastic job."

Suzie nodded, still taking in the impressive changes. "Absolutely. It's more than I ever expected. I think we made the right choice by trusting him with this. It feels like we're stepping into a new chapter."

The twins spent the rest of the day exploring every corner of the workshop, chatting with Elfin about the improvements, and discussing their next steps. They were filled with renewed hope and excitement for the future, reassured that their business was in capable hands and ready to take on new challenges.

Elfin presented them with a particularly remarkable item—a broken wooden chair that, in its prime, would have been a luxurious piece of furniture. The chair, with its elegant carvings and rich, polished finish, now showed signs of wear and damage. It bore a label that read, "To repair and then donate to a local charity for fundraising."

"This chair, once repaired, could be worth thousands of dollars," Elfin said with a hint of pride, his eyes scanning the intricate design and rare timber used. "Look at the craftsmanship. The wood itself is something special—perhaps oak or mahogany. It's a piece with a history and value beyond its current state. All these broken items were left by townspeople, many accompanied by notes or instructions. They've entrusted us with their memories and their generosity."

He paused, allowing the gravity of his words to sink in. "It's not just about fixing things. It's about preserving the past and giving these objects a second life. It's a privilege and a responsibility."

The twins, Sandy and Suzie, exchanged glances, feeling the weight of their new responsibility. Elfin's words were both inspiring and daunting. He then offered his congratulations on their graduation, which marked the beginning of their practical journey into the world of repairs and charity. "You've done well, and now it's time to put your skills to the test," he encouraged them. "Get to work and make every piece shine."

The repaired items soon looked better than new. Every scratch was smoothed, every seam was reinforced, and each toy was polished to perfection. The transformation was remarkable, and the twins felt a growing sense of accomplishment with each finished piece. They loaded the truck with the mended toys and furniture, setting out on their first delivery with the new vehicle.

The truck, a shining new model, was emblazoned with the letters 'XMAS' in gold on both sides and the rear. The glittering letters were not just festive; they also represented a blend of the twins' names—Xavier and Merry Susan. The truck was a symbol of their venture and the Christmas season that was fast approaching.

The delivery process turned out to be more challenging than they had expected. Navigating the truck through the narrow, winding streets of the town required patience and skill. The 'XMAS' truck was a constant reminder of the holiday season, which meant that demand for toy repairs was increasing. Every corner they turned, every bump they encountered, was a test of their ability to handle the load and the logistics.

As they made their way through the town, Elfin guided them with practical advice. "Remember, communication is key," he said during one of their breaks. "Keep the customers informed about their deliveries. It builds trust and ensures that they feel valued. And always handle the items with care—each one has its own story."

The twins took his words to heart. They approached each delivery with a sense of purpose and professionalism. At each stop, they carefully unloaded the items, making sure to handle them with the utmost care. They greeted each customer warmly, explaining the repairs that had been made and answering any questions. The interactions were a learning experience in themselves, teaching them the importance of customer service and attention to detail.

The truck seemed almost bottomless, able to accommodate an astonishing amount of goods. They quickly realized that the logistics of loading and unloading were more complex than they had anticipated. Every item had to be carefully arranged to maximize space and prevent damage. They spent several days mastering the process, learning to navigate the truck's storage efficiently.

In addition to their practical skills, the twins began to appreciate the nuances of customer relations. They learned to listen actively, empathize with customers, and provide solutions to any issues that arose. Each delivery became an opportunity to refine their craft and build connections within the community.

As Christmas drew nearer, the demand for toy repairs intensified. The twins, now more confident and skilled, embraced the challenge with enthusiasm. They continued to work tirelessly, driven by the knowledge that their efforts were making a difference in people's lives.

Before returning to school, the twins reflected on their journey so far. They had come a long way from their initial uncertainties. The experience had not only taught them the technical aspects of repairs but also the importance of dedication, teamwork, and compassion. They were proud of what they had accomplished and eager to continue their work, knowing that each repair was a step towards spreading holiday cheer and helping those in need.

As November approached, Elfin gave the twins an important piece of advice. With Christmas approaching rapidly, he suggested they inform their customers that all repairs and requests should be placed in a safe location, such as on the front porch or in front of the garage. He stressed the importance of setting a deadline, marking November 15th as the last day for pickups. This timeline would provide enough time to handle repairs and ensure that everything was delivered before Christmas Eve.

The twins, initially taken aback by the tight deadline, were skeptical about meeting it. The idea of handling the volume of work within such a short time frame seemed nearly impossible. However, Elfin was resolute. "Trust me," he said with a reassuring smile. "We've got this. With the help of our dedicated volunteers, we can meet our promises." His confidence was contagious, and the twins found themselves willing to give it a try.

By early November, the situation had become overwhelming. The influx of customers had been staggering, and the workshop was bursting at the seams. Items for repair were piled up everywhere, and there was barely any room left to accommodate new requests. The twins were running out of space and were beginning to feel the pressure.

In response to the burgeoning workload, Elfin proposed a solution. "We need a larger space," he declared. He pointed to a much bigger building adjacent to their current factory. This building had been lying dormant since World War II, where it had once served as a storage facility for war supplies. The twins eyed the structure warily. Its size and condition seemed daunting, and they were concerned about the potential costs involved.

Elfin, ever the problem-solver, was quick to reassure them. "Don't worry about the costs," he said confidently. "I have connections that can help. I know someone in the Defense Department who might be able to assist us." The twins were curious but still uncertain. They wondered how someone in the Defense Department could be of help in their situation.

As it turned out, Elfin's assurances were spot-on. The Defense Department had no further use for the warehouse and had planned to demolish it. However, recognizing the building would be repurposed for charitable activities, they agreed to lease it to the twins' workshop for a nominal fee of $1.00 per year. The twins could hardly believe their luck. It was an incredibly generous offer, and they were ecstatic about the opportunity.

Despite their excitement, the twins were still anxious about the looming deadlines. The volume of inquiries and requests from across the United States felt almost insurmountable. They were overwhelmed, feeling as though they had bitten off more than they could chew.

Elfin, however, was undeterred. He approached the situation with his characteristic optimism. "The warehouse needs a bit of work," he explained. "We'll need to fix broken windows, add a fresh coat of paint, and set up basic facilities like electricity and water." He assured them that he had contacts who could handle these tasks swiftly.

True to his word, the renovation work was completed with astonishing speed. What was originally estimated as a two-month job was wrapped up in just two days. The site was abuzz with activity as workers diligently addressed each task. The sound of hammers and drills was accompanied by lively singing and whistling, a testament to their dedication and camaraderie.

Elfin himself took on the role of project manager, overseeing the entire process. His presence was a constant source of motivation and efficiency. "Everything's going according to plan," he would report to the twins, his tone filled with encouragement. "We're making great progress!"

The twins watched in amazement as the once-dilapidated building transformed into a functional workspace. The rapid progress was a testament to the skill and commitment of everyone involved. As the renovations neared completion, the twins felt a renewed sense of hope. With the new warehouse ready, they could finally address the backlog of repairs and meet their Christmas deadlines.

Elfin's unwavering support and the collective effort of the volunteers had turned what seemed like an impossible situation into a manageable one. The twins were grateful for the opportunity and were eager to tackle the tasks ahead. The holiday season was approaching, and they were more determined than ever to fulfill their promises and spread some Christmas cheer.

The collaboration and dedication shown by everyone involved served as a reminder of the power of community and the spirit of giving. With the new space ready and their resolve strengthened, the twins were prepared to face the challenges ahead and ensure that the holiday season would be a joyous one for all their customers.

When the work was finally finished, the twins could hardly believe their eyes. The warehouse, once filled with piles of unorganized toys and scattered tools, now gleamed with order and efficiency. The toys were neatly arranged, ready for the upcoming tasks. The air was filled with a sense of accomplishment and anticipation. Elfin, the head of the team, gathered Sandy and Suzie together with a warm smile.

"Sandy and Suzie," he said, his voice carrying a tone of gentle authority, "it's time to start our work. We have many Christmas promises to fulfill, and there's quite a lot to do."

He glanced at the clock on the wall, which read only 3:00 PM. Elfin, noticing their weariness, suggested, "Why don't you both take a little rest? There's still plenty of time to get ready for what's coming next."

The twins, feeling an unexpected wave of fatigue sweep over them, nodded in agreement. They found a cozy corner with a pair of soft, comfortable beds that Elfin had set up just for them. The room was warm and inviting, with the faint scent of pine from the nearby Christmas trees. As they settled into the beds, the gentle hum of the warehouse's machinery and the soft chatter of Elfin's team provided a soothing backdrop. Soon, they drifted into a deep, restful sleep, their dreams filled with images of toys and festive cheer.

The following morning, Sandy and Suzie awoke to the sound of bustling activity. Elfin and his team were already hard at work, preparing for the next phase of their mission. The warehouse was alive with energy as the dwarfs moved about with purpose. Elfin, who stood at about five foot two, looked every bit the leader with his crisp, red uniform and twinkling eyes. His helpers, all dwarfs, moved efficiently, organizing the various items with precision.

As the twins rubbed the sleep from their eyes and stretched their limbs, Elfin approached them with a bright smile. "Good morning, Sandy and Suzie," he greeted them cheerfully. "Today, we're going to introduce you to the next step of our work. We need to start collecting toys and other items from across the USA, Canada, and Mexico."

With a dramatic flourish, Elfin whistled sharply. The sound echoed through the warehouse, and moments later, a large, enclosed sled appeared as if by magic. It was a magnificent sight, gleaming with festive decorations and perfectly prepared for its journey. The sled was drawn by eight majestic reindeer, each one adorned with colorful harnesses.

Elfin pointed to the reindeer and introduced them. "These are our reindeer: Dasher, Dancer, Prancer, Vixen, Comet, Cupid, Donder, and Blitzen," he said, gesturing to each one in turn. The reindeer, with their shiny antlers and bright eyes, seemed to nod in acknowledgment of the twins' presence.

"Let's show the twins how it's done," Elfin continued with enthusiasm. "We'll start slowly today as they learn the ropes. It's important for them to understand the process."

As the sun dipped below the horizon, casting a golden glow across the snowy landscape, the sled, drawn by the reindeer, began its journey. The reindeer pranced and stamped, their hooves making a soft crunching sound on the snow. The sled glided smoothly, the bells on the reindeer's harnesses jingling merrily.

The news of their mission quickly spread across the North American continent. Families everywhere began to hear about the incredible offer to repair cherished toys and furniture. The excitement was palpable, and the anticipation built up as people eagerly awaited the arrival of the special sled.

Sandy and Suzie, sitting snugly in the sled with Elfin and his team, felt a mix of awe and determination. The night sky was a canvas of twinkling stars, and the snow-covered landscape stretched out in a shimmering blanket below. The adventure had only just begun, and the twins were ready to embrace the challenges ahead. They were eager to make the most of their newfound opportunities and contribute to the magic of the season.

Elfin's voice cut through the crisp night air, filled with a sense of encouragement. "Remember, every toy we repair and every piece of furniture we restore brings joy to a child and warmth to a home. We're not just working; we're spreading Christmas cheer."

The sled continued its journey, cutting through the night with purpose. The twins looked out at the vast expanse before them, their hearts brimming with excitement and hope. They knew that this was just the beginning of a remarkable adventure, one that would test their resilience and dedication. But they were ready, ready to take on the challenges and make a difference, one toy at a time.

Chapter 11
A MAGICAL JOURNEY

The reindeer, confident and assured in their journey, paused occasionally as Elfin guided Sandy and Suzie along their path. With a warm and reassuring tone, Elfin said, "You don't need to worry about where we're headed. The reindeer are highly skilled and familiar with every corner of the world. They've been performing this role for many years."

Elfin's eyes sparkled with enthusiasm as he continued, "This year is special because we've introduced a new service, and you two are the very first to be involved in it. It's quite an honor and a privilege."

The reindeer gently came to a halt near Niagara Falls, a majestic spectacle of nature. The falls roared with a mix of triumph and tranquility, the water cascading down with powerful grace. Under the winter sun, the water glistened, creating a stunning contrast against the icy landscape. Elfin took a moment, allowing Sandy and Suzie to fully appreciate the grandeur of the scene before them.

Elfin gestured towards the falls and said, "Look at this magnificent sight. It's moments like these that remind us of the beauty and wonder of the world we live in. I hope you're beginning to realize that something truly special is unfolding for you, and it's intricately tied to Christmas."

With a knowing smile, Elfin added, "You might think of me as Santa's helper, and you'd be right. Santa, our big boss, has his second-in-command, Rudy. As for me, I manage the day-to-day operations of Christmas, ensuring everything runs smoothly and magically."

Elfin then turned his attention back to the reindeer, giving them a gentle command to continue. "Now, we're heading to the North Pole. There, you'll have the chance to meet the great man himself, Santa Claus. He has an important story to share with you, one that will be crucial for the journey ahead."

As they traveled, the landscape changed from the familiar sights of Niagara Falls to the snowy expanses leading towards the North Pole. The reindeer's rhythmic trot was comforting, and the air grew crisper with each passing moment. Sandy and Suzie looked around, their excitement growing with each mile.

After a while, they arrived at the North Pole, which was a wonderland of shimmering snow and twinkling lights. The North Pole was adorned with decorations and bustling with activity. Elfin led them through a pathway lined with candy cane lamps, and the scent of gingerbread and peppermint filled the air.

"Welcome to the North Pole!" Elfin announced with pride. "Here, Christmas magic is at its peak, and everything you see is part of making the holiday season special for everyone around the world."

They walked through a large archway into Santa's workshop, a place of organized chaos filled with elves busy at work. Elfin guided them through the workshop, showing them the various areas where toys were crafted and gifts were carefully wrapped. The elves paused their work to wave and smile at Sandy and Suzie, their faces beaming with the joy of the season.

At the heart of the workshop stood Santa Claus, a jolly figure with a bushy white beard and a red suit. Santa was busy checking his list but looked up with a hearty laugh as Elfin and the girls approached.

"Ho, ho, ho!" Santa greeted warmly. "Elfin, my trusted helper! And who do we have here?"

"These are Sandy and Suzie," Elfin introduced them. "They are the special guests I told you about. This year, they're involved in something new and exciting."

Santa's eyes twinkled with merriment as he extended a hand to the girls. "Welcome, Sandy and Suzie! It's a pleasure to meet you. I've been looking forward to sharing something important with you both."

Santa led them to a cozy corner of the workshop, where a large map of the world was spread out. He pointed to various locations marked with bright, colorful pins.

"This map," Santa explained, "shows all the places we need to visit on Christmas Eve. Each pin represents a special location where a Christmas miracle is needed. This year, we have a unique challenge that requires a special touch."

Sandy and Suzie listened intently, their eyes wide with curiosity and awe. Santa continued, "Your involvement this year will help us ensure that every child, no matter where they are, feels the magic of Christmas. It's a big responsibility, but I have faith in both of you."

Elfin nodded in agreement. "Santa believes in you both, and so do I. The journey ahead will be filled with wonder and learning. Remember, you're not alone. The reindeer and all of us are here to support you."

Santa gave them a reassuring smile. "I have no doubt you'll rise to the occasion. Now, let's get ready. The preparations are almost complete, and soon we'll be ready to embark on this magical journey."

With that, the room filled with a sense of excitement and anticipation. Sandy and Suzie felt a mix of nerves and exhilaration, ready to take on their special roles in the grand celebration of Christmas.

With a sudden burst of speed, the reindeer soared into the sky, their hooves barely making a sound as they glided through the crisp, wintry air. The night was clear and the stars twinkled like diamonds against the velvet sky. Moments later, they descended gracefully, landing outside a charming log cabin nestled deep in the heart of the North Pole wilderness. The cabin, bathed in the soft glow of the moonlight, was adorned with festive decorations that sparkled and shimmered, casting a warm, inviting glow against the snowy backdrop.

As the sleigh came to a stop, a tall man with shaggy hair and a prominent red nose emerged from the cabin. His clothing, made of coarse brown material, was perfectly suited for the harsh northern winter. Despite his rugged appearance, he wore a broad, warm smile that seemed to instantly make the cold night a little warmer. His eyes, twinkling with kindness, surveyed the arriving guests with a look of genuine enthusiasm.

Elfin, dressed in his traditional green and red attire, shook hands with Rudy, who had taken the reins of the sleigh with great skill. Turning towards the man in red, Elfin said, "Hi, Boss. You've made a splendid choice for your new project. Allow me to introduce you to Sandy and Suzie."

The man in red extended his hand, his grin widening. "I don't believe in formality," he said with a friendly chuckle. "Actions speak louder than words. You can call me Nick. While you're a bit too young to share a glass of wine with me, a hot chocolate should suffice."

Sandy and Suzie, their faces lit up with curiosity and excitement, shook Nick's hand. "It's a pleasure to meet you, Nick," Sandy said, her voice filled with a mix of anticipation and nervousness.

Nick's smile grew even warmer as he motioned them inside. The living room was a cozy haven, with a roaring fire crackling in the hearth. The scent of pine and cinnamon filled the air, mingling with the rich aroma of freshly baked cookies. Soft, comfortable chairs were arranged around the fireplace, and the room was adorned with twinkling lights and festive garlands.

"Christmas is only seven weeks away," Nick began, his voice taking on a tone of urgency tempered with excitement. He gestured for them to sit down, and they settled into the plush chairs, feeling the warmth of the fire on their faces. "There's much work to be done," he continued, his eyes gleaming with enthusiasm. "But before we dive into that, let me tell you a story."

As the flames danced in the fireplace, Nick recounted the tale of Sandy and Suzie's parents and grandparents. His voice was gentle and respectful, each word carefully chosen to honor their memory. He spoke of their remarkable resilience and unwavering spirit, painting a vivid picture of the love and strength that had defined their family. The room was silent except for the crackling of the fire, as Sandy and Suzie listened intently, feeling a mixture of pride and sorrow.

After the story, Nick's expression grew more serious. "Now, let's talk about the new service we're introducing this year," he said. His tone shifted to one of excitement as he introduced the groundbreaking initiative. "This year, we're going to add something special. It involves reusing broken toys and some cherished furniture items. These are not just any items; they hold memories and magic of their own."

He paused for a moment, letting the weight of his words sink in. "While the traditional delivery of Christmas gifts will continue unchanged, this new project will bring a new layer of magic and renewal. We're going to breathe new life into these beloved items, giving them a second chance to spread joy."

Sandy's eyes widened with wonder. "That sounds amazing!" she exclaimed. "How will it work?"

Nick's face lit up with enthusiasm. "We'll take these old toys and furniture, repair them, and infuse them with a bit of Christmas magic. It's all about preserving the memories and creating something beautiful out of what might otherwise be forgotten."

Suzie, her curiosity piqued, leaned forward. "And how can we help?"

Nick's eyes twinkled with approval. "Your involvement will be crucial. We need your creativity and enthusiasm to make this project a success. There will be many tasks to undertake, from sorting through the items to adding the final touches of magic. Together, we can make this Christmas unforgettable for many families."

Elfin nodded in agreement. "It's a big task, but I know you two are up to the challenge," he said, giving Sandy and Suzie an encouraging smile.

Nick clapped his hands together, a gesture that seemed to signal the beginning of something exciting. "Alright then, let's get started. We've got a lot of work ahead of us, but with your help, I'm confident that this will be the most magical Christmas yet."

As the evening progressed, the room filled with the sounds of laughter and the clinking of mugs as Nick served hot chocolate. The warmth of the drink seemed to mirror the warmth of their growing camaraderie. Sandy and Suzie felt a renewed sense of purpose and excitement, knowing that they were about to embark on a truly special journey.

Elfin and the reindeer faced a considerable workload, but Nick's confidence in Sandy and Suzie's capabilities was clear. With a reassuring smile, he posed a question, "Do you think you can meet the challenge?"

"Yes, we definitely can!" Sandy and Suzie responded in unison, their voices filled with determination and enthusiasm.

"Nick," they added gratefully, "thank you for trusting us."

Nick nodded approvingly, his eyes shining with encouragement. "You've got a busy night ahead of you. Make sure to familiarize yourselves with the landscape. There are many items to repair before Christmas Day."

With their farewells said, Elfin took the lead, guiding Sandy and Suzie through a whirlwind tour of the North American continent. As the sun began to rise, casting a soft glow over the snowy landscape, Elfin gave a sharp whistle. In response, two sleds appeared, each drawn by a team of four reindeer. The sight was both impressive and daunting, a testament to the enormity of the task at hand.

The sleds, brimming with potential, awaited the cousins' efforts. The task before them was substantial, but Sandy and Suzie were undeterred. They began their work, visiting house after house, each one a unique stop on their journey. Broken gifts were carefully collected and placed into the sleds. The sleds, though appearing ordinary from the outside, held a magical quality within them. They seemed to possess an almost limitless storage capacity, reminiscent of the TARDIS from Doctor Who.

Sandy and Suzie were awestruck by the seemingly infinite space inside the sleds. They marveled at how time seemed to stretch in extraordinary ways, as if they were in a realm where the usual constraints did not apply. Their work continued with a sense of wonder and determination. Although time appeared to move at an astonishing pace, their efforts seemed to fit perfectly into the rhythm of the night.

Hours passed swiftly as they went about their work, their actions becoming almost instinctive. The quiet of the night was punctuated only by the soft crunch of snow underfoot and the occasional jingle of the reindeer's harnesses. They felt a sense of accomplishment with each repaired item, knowing that their efforts were contributing to a greater purpose.

During a brief pause, Sandy and Suzie huddled together, sharing a moment of respite. Sandy had fallen into a light sleep, and his movement had inadvertently stirred Suzie awake. As they sat together, Sandy's eyes sparkled with excitement. "I just had an amazing dream," he said, his voice tinged with awe. "We were flying through the stars, delivering presents to children all around the world."

Suzie's eyes widened with interest. "Really? That sounds incredible! What happened next?"

Sandy chuckled softly, shaking his head as if trying to recall the details. "It was so vivid. I felt like I could reach out and touch the stars. And then we landed on a magical planet where everything was made of candy. The reindeer were playing in a field of sparkling snow."

Suzie laughed, her excitement matching Sandy's. "That's such a wonderful dream! It's amazing how our imagination can take us to such incredible places."

They exchanged smiles, their spirits buoyed by the shared moment of joy. As they prepared to continue their work, Elfin approached with a nod of approval. "You're doing great," he said. "Keep up the good work. We have a lot more ground to cover."

With renewed energy, Sandy and Suzie resumed their task. They continued visiting homes, their movements becoming more fluid and synchronized as they settled into a rhythm. The reindeer, too, seemed to sense the importance of the mission, their movements steady and purposeful.

As the night wore on, the world outside remained a silent witness to their efforts. The houses they visited were filled with the warm glow of holiday lights, a stark contrast to the cold, snowy exterior. Each home they repaired was a testament to the joy and magic of the season, and Sandy and Suzie felt a deep sense of fulfillment with every gift they restored.

Their journey was not just about repairing broken items; it was a celebration of the holiday spirit and the joy of giving. Sandy and Suzie knew that their efforts were making a difference, and that knowledge kept them motivated throughout the long night.

Eventually, as dawn approached and the first light of morning began to break through the darkness, Sandy and Suzie felt a mixture of exhaustion and satisfaction. They had completed their task with diligence and care, and the sleds were now filled with repaired gifts ready for delivery.

Elfin, observing their progress, gave a satisfied nod. "You've done a fantastic job," he said. "We're almost done. Just a few more houses, and we'll be ready for the final leg of our journey."

With a sense of accomplishment, Sandy and Suzie pressed on, eager to complete their mission. The final homes were visited with the same enthusiasm and care as the first, and as the sun began to rise, casting its golden light over the snowy landscape, they knew they had achieved something truly special.

As they completed their last stop, Sandy and Suzie exchanged one final look of triumph. Their hard work had paid off, and the magic of Christmas would continue to shine brightly for children all around the world.

"Did you?" Suzie asked, her eyes wide with curiosity. "What was it about?"

Before Elfin could respond, he reappeared with a spring in his step and a bright, cheerful expression. "It's ten after three, and tomorrow is shaping up to be the busiest day yet," he announced, his voice bubbling with excitement.

Sandy and Suzie, still processing the surreal experience of their nap, looked at Elfin with a mix of wonder and anticipation. Elfin's eyes twinkled mischievously as he continued, "Did you enjoy your nap? What do you think of the reindeer and the great man?"

The twins exchanged glances, their words momentarily lost as they tried to grasp the reality of their situation. Their faces reflected a blend of amazement and disbelief. Finally, with a shared nod of agreement, they followed Elfin outside, their hearts pounding with a mixture of excitement and nervousness.

The crisp, cold air hit them as they stepped out. The scene before them was even more enchanting than before. Two grand sleds stood in the snow, each magnificently adorned and pulled by four majestic reindeer. The reindeer, with their antlers reaching high into the sky, looked both regal and serene. The sleighs themselves sparkled in the twilight, their bright colors and intricate designs reflecting the last rays of the setting sun.

Elfin's voice carried a hint of amusement as he broke the silence. "You know that what you experienced was no dream," he said, a playful grin spreading across his face. "How would you like to continue with the job you just had?"

The twins' eyes widened with enthusiasm. "Oh, yes please!" they replied in unison, their voices full of eager anticipation.

Elfin's face lit up with approval. "Then don't just stand there," he said, clapping his hands together with a crisp, satisfying sound. "Get to work, and welcome to the wonderful world of Nicholas Claus."

With Elfin's encouragement ringing in their ears, Sandy and Suzie felt a surge of renewed energy and excitement. They glanced at each other, their faces reflecting a shared sense of wonder and readiness for the adventure ahead. The thrill of embracing the magic and responsibility of their new roles filled them with a vibrant energy.

As they approached the sleds, the air around them seemed to hum with possibility. The reindeer, sensing their presence, shifted their stance and nuzzled the twins gently, as if acknowledging their new companions. Sandy and Suzie eagerly began to prepare the sleds, their hands moving with a newfound sense of purpose. They carefully checked the harnesses, ensuring everything was in perfect order for the journey that lay ahead.

Elfin watched them with satisfaction, his eyes sparkling with pride. "You're going to do wonderfully," he said encouragingly. "This is a special time, and you're a crucial part of making it all happen."

With each passing moment, the excitement grew. Sandy and Suzie, now fully immersed in their roles, embraced the magic of their surroundings. They felt a deep sense of responsibility and joy, knowing that they were part of something truly extraordinary. The night sky above them was clear and filled with stars, casting a gentle glow over the snowy landscape and adding to the enchanting atmosphere of the evening.

As they continued their preparations, the anticipation of the coming day's adventure filled them with an exhilarating sense of purpose. They were ready to dive into the extraordinary journey ahead, eager to embrace the magic and responsibility that awaited them in the wonderful world of Nicholas Claus.

Chapter 12

A New Adventure Begins

The first light of dawn struggled to break through the thick canopy of snowy trees as Sandy and Susan stirred awake, signaling the start of another day. The air was crisp, their breaths visible as clouds of mist in the early morning cold. With sleepy but eager movements, they began their morning routine, donning layers upon layers of warm clothing. The chill in the air was biting, but nothing could diminish their excitement. Today would be another adventure in their new magical endeavor.

As they stepped outside, the scene around them was peaceful yet brimming with quiet anticipation. The two sleds, adorned with festive ribbons and decorations, stood ready by the barn. The reindeer stamped their hooves into the snow, their impatience evident as they waited to begin the day's journey. These were no ordinary reindeer, of course. The energy they radiated hinted at something magical, and they were eager to get moving.

Elfin, their whimsical guide and mentor, was already waiting for them by the barn door. His eyes twinkled with mischief and magic, always the first to brighten their spirits no matter how cold it got.

Dressed in his usual quirky attire—a mismatched collection of scarves, hats, and gloves—he seemed immune to the weather's bite.

"Good morning, girls," he said, his voice filled with cheer. "Today, we're heading out to the Midwest. We've got quite a few families eagerly awaiting the return of their repaired toys and furniture. It's going to be a busy day, so we'll need to work quickly and efficiently."

Sandy and Susan exchanged excited glances, their breath visible in the cold air. This was what they had signed up for—delivering joy, one restored item at a time. It hadn't been long since they'd first embarked on this magical journey, but each day had been an adventure in its own right. Every morning brought new challenges, rewards, and unforgettable experiences. Just the day before, they had managed to repair an impressive number of broken toys and cherished items, more than they had anticipated. The look of joy on the faces of the families they helped made every bit of effort worth it.

The adventure began as they hitched the reindeer to their sleds and set out through the snowy landscape. The cold nipped at their noses, but the excitement of the journey warmed them from within. They traveled over vast fields blanketed in snow, through forests that sparkled in the morning light, and past small towns that were just beginning to wake up. The twins marveled at the beauty of the world around them, but they never lost sight of their task.

As they approached their first stop, a quaint little neighborhood with snow-covered cottages, the air seemed to buzz with anticipation. They had been here before, collecting toys and furniture that needed repairs, and now they were back to deliver them, better than new. Sandy and Susan unloaded the first batch of items with care, making sure that every piece was handled with the utmost attention.

The families' reactions were priceless. Some children squealed with delight upon seeing their favorite toys restored, while parents gasped at the sight of furniture pieces they had assumed were beyond saving. A particularly memorable moment was when a small boy, barely five years old, hugged a teddy bear that had been missing an arm for years. Now, the bear was whole again, and the child's gratitude was boundless.

Not all deliveries were met with such emotional outbursts, though. Some families were more subdued, surprised at receiving items they had long forgotten. One elderly couple had completely forgotten they had given the twins a wooden rocking chair that had been passed down through generations. When they saw the restored chair, the wife's eyes filled with tears. "I thought we'd lost this forever," she whispered, running her hand along the smooth wood.

The twins didn't just deliver these repaired items; they delivered memories. Every toy, every piece of furniture held sentimental value, and they took great care to honor that. While Sandy focused on unloading and arranging the items, Susan made sure each delivery was accompanied by a heartfelt note. "We're so happy we could help," the notes always read. "May this item bring as much joy as it once did." These simple messages often brought smiles to the families' faces, a small but meaningful touch that made the twins' work even more special.

As the day went on, the stops became more frequent, and the work more demanding. The sleds were emptied and refilled with new repair requests, but Sandy and Susan never let their enthusiasm wane. The gratitude they saw in each family's eyes was more than enough to keep them going, despite the physical toll of the long hours.

Their journey took them through neighborhoods that varied in size and appearance, from quaint cottages to grand, festively decorated houses. Each place had its unique charm, and the twins reveled in the diversity of the families they met. At one stop, they delivered a delicate porcelain doll to a little girl who hugged it as though she would never let go. At another, they restored a beloved family dining table, and the homeowners were stunned into silence at its pristine condition.

The long hours in the freezing cold would have been daunting if not for the warmth they felt from the families' appreciation. By the time the sun began to dip low in the sky, casting a golden glow over the snow-covered landscape, the twins were both tired and satisfied. Their sleds were once again full, but this time with a new set of repair requests from the families they had visited. It was a never-ending cycle, but one that filled them with purpose.

When they finally returned to their temporary workshop, exhaustion began to set in. The day had been long and physically demanding, but they felt accomplished. Elfin was there to greet them as they stepped inside, his smile as bright as ever. "Well done today, girls," he said, handing them each a steaming mug of hot cocoa. The rich, sweet aroma filled the room, and the warmth of the drink was an instant comfort.

"You're becoming quite adept at this," Elfin continued, his tone both proud and encouraging. "But remember, we've still got a lot of work ahead of us before Christmas."

Sandy and Susan exchanged weary but contented smiles as they sipped their cocoa. The tiredness that had been weighing down their limbs melted away, replaced by a sense of accomplishment. They had worked hard today, but they knew there was still much more to be done. The thought didn't discourage them; it only strengthened their resolve.

As they settled into the cozy workshop to begin their tasks for the evening, the twins couldn't help but reflect on how far they had come. When this magical adventure had begun, they had been excited but unsure of what to expect. Now, they were navigating their new responsibilities with growing skill and confidence. The repair work was not always easy, and the long hours often left them exhausted, but the joy they brought to others made it all worthwhile.

Their father had always believed in the power of kindness and hard work, and it was his legacy they were honoring with every item they repaired. He had taught them to appreciate the sentimental value of things, to understand that a simple toy or piece of furniture could hold a lifetime of memories. And now, they were passing that lesson on to the families they served.

The night settled in around them, and the snow outside continued to fall softly. Inside, the warmth of the workshop and the rhythm of their work kept the twins focused. The hours stretched on, but their dedication never wavered. They carefully repaired each item, preparing it for the next round of deliveries. With every toy they fixed and every piece of furniture they restored, they felt a deep sense of purpose.

As the night grew later, they finally took a moment to rest. The snow-covered landscape outside was bathed in the soft glow of the moon, and for a brief moment, everything felt peaceful and still. But even as they paused, their minds were already turning to the next day. There were more families to help, more items to repair, and they were ready for whatever challenges lay ahead.

Their magical journey had transformed from a whimsical adventure into something much deeper—a mission to spread joy and preserve memories. They had embraced their roles with enthusiasm, knowing that each day brought them closer to fulfilling their mission and honoring their father's memory in the most meaningful way possible.

As they finally retired for the night, the twins knew they were far from finished. But with each passing day, they were becoming more skilled, more confident, and more determined than ever. And that knowledge was enough to carry them through whatever lay ahead.

Chapter 13

Unexpected Challenges

As the days swiftly flew by, Sandy and Suzie were engulfed in a whirlwind of activity. The approach of Christmas brought a flurry of tasks that required their full attention and energy. The twins, who had already grown accustomed to their work, faced each day with increasing skill and confidence. They had become quite adept at managing their responsibilities, but with every passing hour, new and unexpected challenges emerged, putting their resolve to the test.

The surge in workload as Christmas approached was nothing short of dramatic. The workshop was alive with activity, the once orderly environment now buzzing with constant motion. The reindeer, ever-vigilant and steadfast, labored tirelessly, their hooves and harnesses moving in synchronized rhythm to meet the escalating demands. What was once a manageable amount of work had now become a massive undertaking, with each day presenting its own unique hurdles.

One particularly chilly evening, the twins found themselves grappling with a particularly daunting pile of repairs. The cold air seeped through the workshop's walls, making the task at hand even more challenging. Sandy and Suzie were deep in concentration, their hands moving efficiently as they worked through the repairs, when their focus was abruptly interrupted by Elfin's urgent arrival. His usual cheerful demeanor was replaced with a look of genuine concern, his brows furrowed as he approached the twins.

"We've hit a snag," Elfin said, his voice tinged with palpable worry. The urgency in his tone was unmistakable. "The North Pole workshop has reported a shortage of materials. We need to find a solution quickly, or some of the repairs might not be completed in time."

The twins' faces fell as they processed the gravity of the situation. Sandy's eyes widened with concern, and Suzie bit her lip, her thoughts racing. The thought of not meeting their deadlines was disheartening, but the twins were determined not to let this obstacle derail their progress. They had come too far and worked too hard to let something like this stand in their way.

"How bad is it?" Sandy asked, her voice steady despite her rising anxiety. She glanced at Suzie, who was already organizing the scattered tools on their workbench.

Elfin took a deep breath, trying to steady himself. "The shortage is quite severe. We're talking about a significant reduction in the materials we need to complete the repairs. If we don't find a solution soon, we might not be able to meet the Christmas deadline."

Suzie straightened up, her mind already racing through possible solutions. "What can we do to help? Is there any way we can get more materials, or do we have to find an alternative?"

Elfin nodded, a glimmer of hope in his eyes. "There might be a way. We could reach out to some of our suppliers in the neighboring towns.

They might have some excess stock or be able to provide us with what we need. But we'd have to act fast."

Sandy and Suzie exchanged determined glances. They knew the importance of the task at hand and the potential consequences of failing to address the shortage. Without hesitation, Sandy spoke up. "We'll start contacting the suppliers right away. We can split the list and work through it systematically. If we can't get what we need from them, we'll think of another solution."

Elfin's face softened with gratitude. "Thank you. I knew I could count on you both. I'll provide you with the contact information for the suppliers and any other details you might need."

As Elfin handed over the list of suppliers, Sandy and Suzie quickly got to work. The workshop, once filled with the sounds of clinking tools and rustling papers, now echoed with the soft hum of phone conversations. Sandy dialed the first number on the list, her voice steady and professional as she explained the situation and inquired about the availability of materials. Suzie, on the other hand, navigated through her calls with equal determination, her focus unwavering as she spoke with various suppliers.

Hours passed, and the tension in the workshop was palpable. Each call was met with either hopeful responses or disappointing news. Despite the setbacks, the twins remained undeterred. They collaborated and strategized, their combined efforts slowly but surely bringing them closer to a solution.

Eventually, after what felt like an eternity, the twins received some positive news. A supplier in a nearby town had a surplus of the materials they needed and was willing to make an urgent delivery. The relief was evident on Sandy and Suzie's faces as they relayed the good news to Elfin.

"We've managed to secure the materials we need," Sandy announced, her voice filled with a mixture of exhaustion and triumph. "They're sending a shipment over, and we should have everything we need within the next few hours."

Elfin let out a sigh of relief, his worry visibly lifting. "That's fantastic news. I can't thank you both enough for your quick thinking and dedication. You've really saved the day."

Suzie smiled, her tired eyes reflecting the satisfaction of a job well done. "It was a team effort. We couldn't have done it without your help and guidance."

As the evening wore on and the workshop buzzed back to its usual rhythm, Sandy and Suzie continued their repairs with renewed vigor. The looming deadline no longer seemed quite as daunting, and the twins felt a renewed sense of hope. They knew that, despite the challenges they faced, their hard work and determination would see them through to a successful Christmas.

Without wasting a moment, Sandy and Suzie sprang into action. The urgency of their situation drove them to act swiftly. They knew that time was of the essence, so they immediately reached out to local suppliers. They carefully crafted their messages, clearly explaining the urgency and importance of their request. They highlighted the approaching Christmas deadline and the critical need for the materials to complete their project. Their tone was earnest and sincere, hoping to convey just how much their work meant to the community and those it would benefit.

Simultaneously, they mobilized a network of volunteers, rallying friends, family members, and community members. They spread the word through social media, local bulletin boards, and personal calls. "We need all hands on deck," Sandy said during one of their many phone calls. "Every bit of help counts, whether it's time, resources, or just spreading the word."

The response from the community was nothing short of incredible. Volunteers of all ages, from eager teenagers to dedicated seniors, came forward. Some offered their time, while others provided resources or assistance with logistics. A group of local high school students organized a toy drive, collecting toys and other materials that were crucial for the repairs. One elderly neighbor, Mrs. Thompson, baked dozens of cookies and brought them to the workshop, offering a sweet treat to keep everyone's spirits high.

The local suppliers were also moved by the twins' dedication and the genuine spirit of the holiday season. They expedited their shipments, ensuring that Sandy and Suzie received the materials they urgently needed. One supplier, Mr. Jensen, who ran the hardware store, personally delivered the supplies to the workshop. "I heard what you're doing," he said, handing over a box of tools. "We're all in this together. Let me know if you need anything else."

As the days grew shorter and the Christmas deadline loomed closer, the twins worked around the clock. Their focus remained unwavering despite the initial setback. The workshop was abuzz with activity, its atmosphere vibrant with the sounds of hammers, screwdrivers, and the occasional burst of laughter. Sandy and Suzie's hands moved deftly, their fingers expertly maneuvering tools as they worked late into the night.

The workshop, once a scene of chaos and concern, had transformed into a hive of activity. Each corner was filled with partially repaired toys and furniture. The walls, lined with shelves of colorful materials, seemed to buzz with the energy of their relentless efforts. Sandy and Suzie would often exchange glances of silent encouragement, their shared resolve shining in their eyes.

The excitement of seeing the repaired items come to life fueled their spirits. Each piece they worked on held a story, a memory, or a cherished place in someone's home. "Look at this old rocking horse," Suzie said one evening, holding up a newly restored toy. "It's going to bring so much joy to a child." Sandy nodded, her face glowing with satisfaction. "Every little bit of effort we put in makes a difference."

As they approached the final stretch, the workshop's atmosphere was electric with a renewed sense of purpose. The twins' commitment was palpable. Each repaired item was carefully inspected and prepared for delivery. Sandy meticulously wrapped toys in festive paper, while Suzie organized the furniture for easy transport. They made sure every detail was attended to, knowing that their hard work would bring smiles and happiness to others.

The anticipation of delivering their work kept them motivated. They often discussed how they imagined the recipients would react, envisioning the joy their efforts would bring. "I can't wait to see their faces," Suzie said with a smile. "It'll all be worth it."

The support from the community had been instrumental in overcoming the material shortage. Sandy and Suzie were deeply grateful for the help they received. They knew that their project had become a collective effort, reflecting the true spirit of Christmas. The collaborative nature of their work underscored values of generosity, kindness, and working together toward a common goal.

As they finished the final touches and prepared for the last deliveries, Sandy and Suzie took a moment to reflect on their journey. They stood together in the workshop, surrounded by the fruits of their labor. "We did it," Sandy said softly, her voice filled with pride. Suzie smiled, her eyes bright with tears of joy. "We really did."

Their hearts were full as they delivered the repaired items, knowing that their hard work and the support of their community had made a meaningful difference. The Christmas season, with all its trials and triumphs, had brought them closer to their neighbors and to each other. The experience had shown them the true power of community and the magic of giving, reaffirming their belief in the goodness that can flourish when people come together.

With each passing day, the twins grew ever closer to achieving their goal. Their tireless efforts were beginning to bear fruit, and the once overwhelming backlog of repairs was steadily diminishing. The workshop, which had previously been cluttered with piles of uncompleted tasks, now stood as a testament to Sandy and Suzie's remarkable resilience and hard work.

As Christmas Eve approached, the atmosphere in the workshop was filled with a palpable sense of excitement. The twins, with their sleeves rolled up and faces smeared with grease from their diligent work, could hardly contain their eagerness. Their anticipation was not just for the approaching holiday but also for the satisfaction of seeing the fruits of their labor come to life. The repairs they had undertaken were nearing completion, and the thought of the joy their work would bring to families across the region filled them with a sense of pride and accomplishment.

Every evening, as the workshop lights flickered on against the encroaching darkness of the winter nights, the twins worked side by side, their teamwork evident in their synchronized movements and shared smiles. Suzie would often hum holiday tunes, which seemed to infuse their labor with a touch of festive spirit, while Sandy meticulously inspected each repaired item, ensuring everything met their high standards. Their conversations were filled with light-hearted banter and mutual encouragement, as they both knew how important their mission was to them and the community.

The challenges they had faced throughout the process had only served to strengthen their resolve. Long hours, unexpected setbacks, and the sheer volume of work had tested their endurance. Yet, each challenge had been met with determination, and their appreciation for the holiday season had deepened significantly. They understood now more than ever the true meaning of giving and the joy of bringing happiness to others.

The support from the community had been a significant factor in their progress. Neighbors, friends, and even strangers had rallied behind them, offering both moral support and practical help. Local businesses had donated materials, and volunteers had pitched in whenever needed. The sense of community spirit was overwhelming, and Sandy and Suzie felt deeply grateful for every helping hand and encouraging word.

With the final stretch toward Christmas in sight, Sandy and Suzie were prepared to give their all. The workshop was now organized and efficient, each completed repair neatly stored and ready for distribution. The sense of accomplishment and fulfillment they felt was immense. It was as if the challenges they had overcome had only added to the value of their work, making the upcoming holiday all the more meaningful.

As they put the finishing touches on their last few repairs, they exchanged glances filled with unspoken understanding. They knew that the real reward lay not just in the completion of their tasks but in the joy their efforts would bring to those who received their gifts. The final push toward Christmas was not merely about finishing their work but about embracing the spirit of the season with enthusiasm and joy.

With each item they finished, Sandy and Suzie could already picture the smiles and hear the laughter that their repairs would inspire. The satisfaction of knowing that their hard work would make a difference in the lives of others was a powerful motivator. They were ready to embrace the holiday season with open hearts, eager to see the impact of their efforts and to celebrate the true spirit of Christmas.

Chapter 14

THE BIG NIGHT APPROACHES

As the days dwindled down to Christmas, a tangible buzz of excitement and urgency permeated the air. The workshop, a hive of activity, thrummed with the sounds of festive preparation. Sandy and Susan, now seasoned and adept in their roles, were at the very center of this whirlwind of holiday cheer, immersed in the critical preparations for the pivotal night ahead.

The workshop, which had once been a mere space for assembling toys, had transformed into a vibrant command center. The clamor of hammering and the clatter of tools filled every corner, blending with the hum of busy voices and the occasional laugh. Volunteers, who had journeyed from distant places, worked alongside Elfin and the reindeer with unwavering dedication. Each person was absorbed in their task, focused on perfecting every detail for the big night.

Elfin, resplendent in his signature festive garb, gathered Sandy and Susan for a crucial briefing. They approached him, their faces a blend of fatigue and exhilaration. Despite the weariness etched into their expressions, their eyes sparkled with anticipation.

"Tonight marks the culmination of all our hard work," Elfin announced, his voice resonating with a mix of pride and gravity. "We've made tremendous progress, but the final deliveries are of the utmost importance. Every toy and piece of furniture we've repaired must reach its destination in perfect condition."

Sandy and Susan exchanged determined glances. They had come a long way since their initial days of uncertainty, their recent experiences having sharpened their skills and bolstered their confidence. Their commitment to ensuring the success of the mission was unwavering. They had mastered the intricacies of toy repair, navigated the complexities of managing a large-scale operation, and reveled in the joy of bringing smiles to countless faces.

Throughout the day, the pair was immersed in meticulous organization. Sandy and Susan moved through the workshop with practiced efficiency, checking each parcel to ensure it was properly packed and accurately labeled. Their hands worked swiftly but with the utmost care, as every toy and piece of furniture was scrutinized for perfection. Each item was a crucial component of the grand puzzle that was Christmas Eve.

As the sun dipped below the horizon, casting a warm, golden glow across the workshop, the reindeer were brought forward. Their harnesses were carefully adjusted, and the sleds were loaded with precision. The reindeer, their coats shimmering in the soft light, seemed to sense the importance of the night ahead. They pranced with a mix of eagerness and patience, their eyes bright with anticipation for the long journey that awaited them.

Sandy and Susan donned their warm, festive gear, their excitement evident in their every movement. The cold, crisp air of the evening heightened their anticipation as they took their positions on the sleds. A surge of adrenaline mixed with a hint of nervousness coursed through them. The night was clear, with stars sparkling overhead as if the universe itself was cheering them on.

Elfin walked over to Sandy and Susan, his expression a blend of encouragement and solemnity. "Remember," he said, placing a reassuring hand on their shoulders, "this is more than just a task. It's about spreading joy and making dreams come true. Every effort you've put in tonight will make a difference."

Sandy nodded, her eyes reflecting a mix of determination and gratitude. "We won't let you down, Elfin. We've come this far, and we're ready."

Susan, her voice steady and resolute, added, "We'll make sure every toy finds its way to the children who need it. We've worked too hard for this to falter now."

Elfin smiled, his eyes twinkling with pride. "I know you will. You've both been incredible throughout this process. Now, let's get everything set for the night ahead."

With a final check of the sleds and a last-minute adjustment to the reindeer harnesses, Sandy and Susan prepared to embark on their journey. The workshop, now quieting down in the final moments before the big night, was a testament to their hard work and dedication. Each corner, each tool, and each toy stood as a reminder of the countless hours spent preparing for this very moment.

As they settled into their positions, the anticipation in the air was almost palpable. The clear night sky, dotted with stars, seemed to promise a successful and magical evening. With the final preparations complete, Sandy and Susan shared one last look, a silent exchange of confidence and resolve.

The reindeer, sensing the beginning of their grand adventure, gave a collective nod, and with a gentle lurch, the sleds began to move. The world outside the workshop awaited their arrival, and the journey to spread Christmas joy was set to begin.

Elfin made his final checks, ensuring that everything was in order for the night ahead. His usual jovial demeanor was tempered with a serious edge as he addressed the twins one last time before they set off.

"Remember," Elfin said, his eyes reflecting the twinkling lights of the workshop, "this night is about more than just delivering presents. It's about spreading joy, hope, and the true spirit of Christmas. Every house you visit, every toy you deliver, represents the love and care we've put into this project. So, stay focused, work as a team, and most importantly, enjoy the journey."

Sandy and Susan nodded, absorbing Elfin's words. They had seen the impact of their work firsthand and understood the significance of their task. The responsibility they carried was immense, but so was their resolve to see it through to the end. They exchanged a glance, a silent understanding passing between them, before turning their attention back to Elfin.

"Are you both ready?" Elfin asked, a hint of encouragement in his voice.

"Ready as we'll ever be," Sandy replied, her tone steady and determined.

Susan smiled, her excitement barely contained. "Let's do this."

The sleds were now fully loaded, the gifts neatly packed and secured. The reindeer, their harnesses shimmering with festive bells, were ready and eager to begin their journey. Elfin took a final look at the list, his eyes scanning for any last-minute adjustments.

With a deep breath and a reassuring nod, Sandy and Susan climbed onto their respective sleds. The workshop fell silent, the only sounds being the soft rustling of the reindeer's harnesses and the gentle murmur of the night. The atmosphere was charged with a sense of anticipation and purpose.

As the clock struck the hour of departure, Elfin gave the signal. With a commanding "Ho, ho, ho!" the reindeer leaped into action, lifting the sleds into the crisp, wintry air. Sandy and Susan held on tight, their hearts pounding with anticipation as the ground below them blurred into a patchwork of lights and shadows.

The initial moments of flight were filled with wonder. The world spread out beneath them like a magical tapestry, illuminated by the shimmering lights of countless homes. Each house they passed seemed to hold a special glow, a beacon of warmth in the cold night. The reindeer soared through the sky with a sense of purpose and grace, their rhythmic hoofbeats creating a gentle melody against the night.

Sandy and Susan marveled at the view. "Look at all the lights," Susan said, her voice filled with awe. "It's like we're flying through a sea of stars."

Sandy nodded, her eyes wide with wonder. "It's amazing. I never imagined it would be like this."

As they approached their first stop, Sandy and Susan's focus sharpened. They worked in perfect unison, unloading the carefully packed gifts and placing them with precision. Their practiced hands moved with a fluid efficiency that came from weeks of preparation. Each movement was deliberate and careful, ensuring that every gift was in the right place.

"Remember to be quiet and quick," Sandy whispered as they moved. "We don't want to wake anyone up."

Susan nodded, her movements steady as she placed the last gift under the tree. "Got it. Let's make sure everything is perfect."

Throughout the night, the twins experienced a blend of awe and exhilaration. Each delivery brought a new sense of accomplishment, and the joy of knowing that their efforts were making a difference fueled their determination. They saw the happiness in the families they visited, the gleam of excitement in children's eyes as they discovered their repaired toys.

At each stop, the twins paused for a moment to take in the scene. The homes, though modest, were filled with warmth and love. They could see the evidence of a family's care in the small details—a carefully decorated tree, handmade ornaments, and stockings hung with care. These moments of quiet reflection reminded them of the true meaning of their mission.

As the night wore on, Sandy and Susan's tiredness was tempered by their sense of accomplishment. The sky began to lighten with the first hints of dawn, but there was no time to rest. They continued their work with the same enthusiasm and dedication, driven by the knowledge that their efforts were making Christmas special for so many people.

"Can you believe how many homes we've visited?" Susan asked, her voice tinged with fatigue but also with pride.

Sandy smiled, her face illuminated by the soft glow of the morning light. "It's incredible. We've done so much already. Just a little more to go."

Their journey continued, each new house adding to their growing sense of fulfillment. The cold night air was now giving way to the warmth of the approaching day, but Sandy and Susan's spirits remained high. They knew that their work was far from over, but they also knew that every delivery brought a little more joy into the world.

As they completed their final stops, Sandy and Susan took a moment to appreciate the beauty of the morning. The first rays of sunlight painted the sky in shades of pink and gold, casting a gentle glow over the snow-covered landscape.

"We did it," Susan said, her voice filled with a mix of exhaustion and triumph.

Sandy nodded, her eyes reflecting the early morning light. "We did. And it was worth every moment."

With their mission accomplished, the twins headed back to the workshop, their hearts full of the joy and satisfaction that comes from making a difference. The journey had been long and challenging, but it was also one they would cherish forever. As they landed back at the workshop, Elfin greeted them with a warm smile and a hearty congratulations.

"Well done, you two," he said, his eyes twinkling with pride. "You've made this Christmas truly special."

Sandy and Susan smiled, their hearts swelling with happiness. They had completed their mission, and in doing so, had experienced the true spirit of Christmas.

Time seemed to stretch and bend in the magical realm they were navigating. The night unfolded with a mix of challenges that tested their resolve and ingenuity. Every twist and turn brought new obstacles, yet

Sandy and Susan faced them with unwavering determination. The cold air nipped at their cheeks, and the long hours began to weigh heavily on their shoulders. Despite this, their spirits remained buoyed by the festive atmosphere and the support of their loyal reindeer. The twinkling lights of the enchanted forest, casting a soft glow over their path, added to the magical quality of their journey.

"Look at that!" Sandy exclaimed, pointing to a shimmering snowflake that floated down from the sky like a tiny star. "I've never seen snowflakes like this before."

Susan smiled, her cheeks flushed with a combination of cold and excitement. "It's beautiful. It's as if the entire world is celebrating with us."

The challenges of the night were met with a combination of careful planning and spontaneous problem-solving. Each stop required not just the delivery of gifts but also attention to detail—ensuring every present was placed perfectly under the tree, every note was personalized, and every home was visited without missing a single detail. They communicated constantly, coordinating their efforts with the reindeer, who knew their roles well and worked diligently to support the twins.

"Remember, every house is unique," Susan reminded Sandy as they approached their next destination. "Let's make sure we take a moment to appreciate each one."

The workload remained heavy, but the twins' enthusiasm never waned. Each new destination was met with renewed energy and focus. They navigated through bustling cities and quiet villages, each location presenting its own set of challenges. Sometimes they had to deal with unexpected weather changes, or they encountered obstacles like tangled decorations and stubborn locks on doors. Through it all, they found solutions with creativity and teamwork.

As they worked, the twins often shared light-hearted conversations to keep their spirits high. "Do you think the reindeer ever get tired?" Sandy asked, glancing at their trusty companions.

Susan laughed softly. "If they do, they're certainly not showing it. They're just as eager as we are to make sure everything is perfect."

The experience was both exhausting and exhilarating, a true test of their skills and endurance. With each completed delivery, they felt a surge of accomplishment. They marveled at the joy and wonder that seemed to permeate every home they visited. The sight of children's eyes lighting up with excitement and the happy chatter of families enjoying their Christmas morning made every effort worthwhile.

With the final deliveries completed, Sandy and Susan made their way back to the workshop just as the first light of dawn began to break. The sky was painted with hues of pink and gold, marking the end of their magical journey. The transition from night to morning was breathtaking, a reminder of the beauty and serenity that followed their hard work.

The workshop was a hive of activity, filled with a sense of accomplishment and joy. The elves and helpers, who had been working tirelessly alongside them, greeted them with cheers and congratulations. The atmosphere buzzed with the energy of a job well done. Elfin, the head elf, clapped Sandy and Susan on the back, his eyes twinkling with pride.

"You did it!" Elfin said, his voice full of admiration. "The deliveries were flawless. We couldn't have done it without you."

Sandy and Susan exchanged a look of satisfaction, their exhaustion melting away in the face of their friends' enthusiasm. The warm embraces and heartfelt congratulations from everyone in the workshop made the long night's work feel even more worthwhile.

As they reflected on their experiences, the twins realized the true meaning of their work. It was not just about delivering presents; it was about spreading love, hope, and the magic of Christmas to families everywhere. Each gift they delivered was a symbol of joy and care, a reminder of the warmth and kindness that defined the holiday season. The journey had been challenging, but it had also been profoundly rewarding, filling them with a deep sense of purpose and fulfillment.

The night had been a testament to their growth and the strength of their partnership. They had faced obstacles with determination, navigated complex situations with skill, and ultimately fulfilled their promise of bringing Christmas magic to life. Their adventure had solidified their bond and deepened their understanding of the holiday's true spirit. They knew that this experience would stay with them forever, shaping their perspectives and their approach to future challenges.

As they prepared to rest, the twins felt a profound sense of fulfillment. The challenges of the night were behind them, but the memories and the impact of their work would remain with them forever. With hearts full of joy and a renewed appreciation for the magic of Christmas, Sandy and Susan looked forward to the future with hope and excitement, knowing that they had made a difference and carried the spirit of the season with them.

Chapter 15
CHRISTMAS MAGIC

The night sky stretched endlessly above, a vast expanse of clear darkness speckled with countless twinkling stars. Each star seemed to shimmer with its own special light, casting a gentle, ethereal glow over the wintry landscape below. The cold December air was crisp and biting, its chill penetrating through layers of clothing, yet it was invigorating, like a bracing splash of cold water on a sleepy face. Despite the cold, Sandy and Susan felt a warm, comforting fire within them—a beacon of determination and excitement.

"This is it, Sandy," Susan said with a mixture of awe and anticipation. Her breath formed small clouds in the frosty air as she spoke. "Our final mission of the season. Can you believe how far we've come?"

Sandy nodded, her eyes reflecting the brilliance of the stars above. "It feels surreal, Susan. All the work we've put in—repaired toys, restored furniture—it's all led up to this. I'm proud of what we've accomplished."

The reindeer, magnificent and strong, soared gracefully through the night sky. Their fur was pristine white, almost glowing against the backdrop of darkness. The antlers, adorned with a gentle sheen of moonlight, added to their regal appearance. Each step they took was accompanied by the soft jingle of bells, their melodic tones weaving through the crisp night air like a lullaby.

As the sleds glided effortlessly through the snow, Sandy and Susan could hear the satisfying crunch of the snow beneath the runners. The sleds were piled high with carefully wrapped packages, each one containing a repaired toy or piece of furniture, meticulously restored by the twins' skilled hands. The packages, wrapped in vibrant, festive paper and adorned with bright ribbons, glistened under the starry sky, adding a splash of color to the otherwise monochromatic scene.

"I still can't get over how these sleds handle the snow," Sandy remarked, adjusting the reins with a practiced touch. "It's like they're practically gliding."

Susan smiled, her eyes twinkling with the reflected light of the stars. "It's not just the sleds. It's our teamwork. We've learned so much about working together and trusting each other. I think that's what makes this all possible."

Their conversation was interrupted by the sound of the reindeer's bells ringing softly. Sandy glanced over at Susan, her face illuminated by the soft glow of the lantern hanging from the sled. "Do you remember the first time we fixed a toy together? It was so challenging, but now it feels like second nature."

Susan laughed softly. "Yes, I remember. We were so worried about getting everything perfect. But look at us now. We've turned that worry into something wonderful. Our mission is more than just delivering these gifts—it's about bringing joy and hope to those who need it most."

As they continued their journey, the sight of the snow-covered landscape stretched out before them, a blanket of white illuminated by the moonlight. The world seemed peaceful and serene, a stark contrast to the bustling activity that awaited them at each stop. The twins worked in perfect harmony, their movements synchronized as they prepared to deliver each carefully wrapped package.

With every stop, the reindeer came to a gentle halt, and Sandy and Susan hopped out of the sleds with practiced ease. They carried the packages with care, ensuring each one was placed exactly where it needed to be. The satisfaction of their task was evident in their smiles and the lightness in their steps.

"This is what it's all about," Susan said as she placed the final package. "Making a difference, one gift at a time."

Sandy nodded in agreement, her heart swelling with pride. "Yes, it is. And knowing that we've helped make someone's holiday a little brighter makes all the hard work worthwhile."

As they resumed their journey, the reindeer's bells jingled merrily in the night, their sound a testament to the success of the mission. The twins' hearts were full, their spirits lifted by the joy they had brought to others. The adventure was far from over, but for now, they took comfort in the knowledge that they had made a difference, and the warmth they felt was a reflection of the love and dedication they had poured into their work.

Every stop on their journey felt like a small moment of magic, a fleeting yet profound experience. As Sandy and Susan approached each home, their hearts quickened with a surge of anticipation. The streets lay quiet beneath the velvety cloak of night, the houses shrouded in serene stillness. Despite the tranquility, there was a palpable sense of excitement in the air, as if the magic of their mission was gently awakening even the most dormant of homes.

"Look at this place," Susan whispered, her voice barely audible over the crunch of snow beneath their boots. "It's like something out of a storybook."

Sandy nodded, her gaze sweeping over the quaint, snow-covered house before them. "It really is. And just think about the joy these packages will bring. It makes everything we've done so worth it."

At one particular house, they carefully placed a beautifully repaired wooden rocking horse on the front porch. The horse, once faded and worn, had been lovingly restored to its former glory. Its paint, now vibrant and new, gleamed softly in the moonlight. Sandy and Susan took a moment to admire their handiwork.

"Imagine the look on a little child's face when they find this," Sandy said, her eyes reflecting the warmth of the lantern's glow. "I bet they'll be over the moon."

Susan smiled, her eyes twinkling with the reflected light of the stars. "I can almost see it now—a child running out, their eyes wide with wonder, and the joy they'll feel. It's moments like these that make everything we do so special."

They moved silently, their movements practiced and precise, always careful not to disturb the quiet of the night. The reindeer stood patiently by the sleds, their breath forming small clouds in the crisp air. Each package was placed with care, as though the twins were handling something precious and delicate.

As they continued their journey, the stars above seemed to guide them, their light reflecting off the snow and creating a path of shimmering white. The twins felt a sense of rhythm in their work, each stop blending seamlessly into the next. It was as if the night itself was orchestrating their adventure, the stars and snow creating a magical tapestry that unfolded with each mile.

The homes they visited were as varied as the decorations that adorned them. Some were adorned with colorful Christmas lights that danced merrily in the night, while others were cozy cottages nestled snugly in snowy drifts. There were also grand houses, their elaborate decorations glittering like a fairy tale come to life. Each location had its own unique charm, and the twins reveled in the simple joy of their task.

"This one's so beautiful," Susan said as they approached a particularly charming house with a row of twinkling lights along the roof. "Look at those lights—they almost look like stars come down to visit."

Sandy smiled, her eyes taking in the festive display. "It's like they're welcoming us. Every house we visit feels like a new chapter in our story, each with its own little bit of magic."

They worked together, moving from house to house, their hearts full of contentment. The joy they felt was a reflection of the happiness they hoped to bring to the families they served. Each moment of their journey was a testament to their dedication and the belief in the power of kindness and generosity.

As the night wore on, the twins continued their journey under the watchful gaze of the stars. The reindeer's bells jingled softly in the night, their sound a comforting reminder of the magic that surrounded them. With each package delivered, the twins felt a renewed sense of purpose, their spirits buoyed by the knowledge that their efforts were making a difference.

With each delivery, Sandy and Susan could see the tangible impact of their work. Toys and furniture that had once been broken and forgotten were now restored to their former glory. The rocking horses, dolls, and chairs, each lovingly repaired, carried with them a piece of the magic that had been woven into them by the twins.

"It's amazing to think about how these things have a second chance," Susan remarked as they carefully placed a beautifully restored toy train under a Christmas tree. "It's like we're giving them a new life, and in turn, giving something special to the families who will use them."

Sandy nodded, her hands deftly adjusting the placement of the train. "I know. Every time I see one of these items, I imagine the joy it will bring to someone. It's like we're spreading a bit of our own magic with every delivery."

As the night wore on, the temperature began to drop, and the snow started to fall more heavily. The gentle flakes swirled gracefully through the air, their descent adding a touch of enchantment to the already magical evening. The snowflakes, illuminated by the soft glow of the moon, seemed to sparkle like tiny stars falling from the sky.

"We're really in the thick of it now," Sandy said, brushing a few flakes off her hat. "The snow is coming down harder, but it makes everything look so beautiful."

Susan smiled, her breath forming little clouds in the chilly air. "It does. It's like we're in a winter wonderland. Even though it's cold, there's something comforting about the snowfall. It makes everything feel so serene."

Wrapped in their warm winter gear, the twins moved with a sense of unity and purpose. Their mission, though challenging and physically demanding, was filled with a profound sense of meaning. Each stop they made, each package they delivered, reinforced the importance of their work.

"Do you think we've done enough?" Susan asked as they paused for a moment, their breath visible in the frosty air. "I mean, I hope we've made a difference."

Sandy looked around at the snowy landscape, her face illuminated by the soft light of their lantern. "I believe we have. Every home we've visited, every item we've restored—it all adds up. We've brought joy and warmth where it was needed, and that's what matters."

As the first light of dawn began to creep over the horizon, the sky slowly shifted from deep navy to soft hues of pink and orange. The sunrise was a breathtaking sight, painting the snow-covered landscape with warm, golden tones. It was a promise of a new day and the culmination of their efforts.

"Look at that," Susan said, her voice filled with awe as she gazed at the emerging sunrise. "It's like the sky is celebrating our success."

Sandy, tired but filled with a sense of accomplishment, nodded in agreement. "It's the perfect ending to our journey. We've done something truly special tonight."

With a final glance at the now softly glowing sky, the twins made their way back to the North Pole. The reindeer, having carried out their duties with grace and strength, were also ready for rest. As they traveled back, the sense of fulfillment and joy from their mission was a comforting presence, warming them even in the early morning chill.

The North Pole awaited them, its familiar glow a welcoming beacon after a long night of hard work. Sandy and Susan knew they would return to the comforts of home, but the memory of their journey and the difference they had made would stay with them, a lasting reminder of the magic they had shared with the world.

The arrival at the North Pole was met with a festive and joyous celebration. The workshop, which had been a hive of activity throughout their journey, now buzzed with an atmosphere of happiness and cheer. The walls echoed with laughter and the clinking of mugs filled with hot cocoa. Elfin, Rudy, and the other helpers, who had been tirelessly working behind the scenes, greeted Sandy and Susan with open arms, their faces alight with pride and joy.

Elfin, his pointy ears twitching with excitement, waved enthusiastically. "You're back! We've been waiting for you!" His voice was filled with genuine delight. Rudy, who had been busy organizing the final batch of toys, paused to join the welcome. "You did it! We heard everything went smoothly. We couldn't be prouder."

The workshop was a scene of warmth and camaraderie. Festive decorations adorned every surface, from garlands draped over the windows to twinkling fairy lights that cast a magical glow. The scent of freshly baked gingerbread cookies and spiced cider filled the air, adding to the celebratory ambiance.

In the center of the celebration stood Nick, dressed in his iconic red suit, his appearance as jolly and reassuring as ever. His eyes sparkled with genuine pride as he approached Sandy and Susan. The sight of him, with his broad smile and cheerful demeanor, was a comforting reminder of the magic that had guided them throughout their journey.

"You've done an incredible job," Nick said, his voice rich with warmth and admiration. He clapped each of them on the shoulder, his touch firm and reassuring. "This has been a year to remember, thanks to your hard work and dedication. I knew you both had something special, and you've proven it with this remarkable mission."

Sandy and Susan exchanged glances, their faces glowing with pride and happiness. "Thank you, Nick," they said in unison, their voices filled with genuine gratitude. "We couldn't have done it without your guidance and the support of everyone here. It was a team effort, and we're so grateful for everything."

Nick's expression softened, his eyes twinkling with the spirit of Christmas. "Remember," he said, his voice imbued with a tender earnestness, "the magic of Christmas is not just about gifts and decorations. It's about the joy we bring to others and the love we share. You've made this Christmas special for so many people. That's the true spirit of the season."

The words resonated deeply with Sandy and Susan. They looked around at the cheerful faces of their friends and the joyful atmosphere that filled the room. The satisfaction of a job well done, combined with the warmth of being surrounded by those who had supported them, created a feeling of contentment that was almost palpable.

The celebration continued with music and dancing. Elfin and Rudy led the festivities, their infectious energy setting the tone for the evening. Sandy and Susan joined in, their hearts full of joy and their spirits lifted by the shared happiness. They laughed, danced, and enjoyed the company of their friends, each moment a testament to the success of their mission.

As the night went on, Sandy and Susan reflected on their journey. They had faced challenges and embraced the magic of the season, and now, they were surrounded by the fruits of their labor. The love and joy they had shared with others had come full circle, enriching their own lives in ways they had never imagined.

As they looked around at the smiling faces and the twinkling lights, Sandy squeezed Susan's hand. "We did it, didn't we? This has been one of the most memorable experiences of our lives."

Susan smiled back, her eyes shining with happiness. "Yes, we did. And I wouldn't have wanted to share it with anyone else. Here's to many more adventures and spreading the magic of Christmas."

And with that, they joined in the celebration, their hearts full and their spirits bright, knowing that they had made a difference and that the magic of Christmas was alive and well, thanks to their hard work and dedication.

As the celebration continued, Sandy and Susan took a quiet moment away from the lively festivities to reflect on their adventure. They stood by a window, looking out at the snow-covered landscape bathed in the soft light of dawn. The view was serene and picturesque, a fitting backdrop for their thoughts.

"It's hard to believe it's over," Sandy said, her voice thoughtful. "It feels like just yesterday we were starting this journey, unsure of what lay ahead."

Susan nodded, her eyes scanning the wintry scene. "It really has been more than just a task. This experience has transformed us in ways I never expected. We've not only fulfilled our mission but discovered something much deeper about Christmas."

The workshop, a hub of festive energy, buzzed with laughter and music. The vibrant sounds of celebration filled the air, each note adding to the joyous atmosphere. The room was adorned with sparkling decorations, twinkling lights, and colorful streamers, all contributing to a scene of pure holiday magic. The cheerful songs that played in the background mirrored the twins' feelings of accomplishment and fulfillment.

As they mingled with the helpers, Sandy and Susan shared stories from their journey, recounting the challenges they had faced and the moments of triumph they had experienced. The helpers listened with interest and admiration, their faces lighting up with pride at the twins' achievements.

"You both have been incredible," Elfin said, his eyes wide with appreciation. "The way you handled everything—it's truly inspiring. You've made this Christmas special for so many people."

Rudy, who had been busy organizing the last of the celebratory treats, nodded in agreement. "Absolutely. You brought so much joy and magic to the world. It's something we'll all remember for years to come."

As the day wore on, the energy of the celebration began to wind down. The laughter grew softer, and the music became a gentle hum in the background. Sandy and Susan, their hearts full and their spirits high, knew that this Christmas would be one they would always cherish. It had been a magical adventure, one that had taught them the true essence of the holiday season.

"We've learned so much," Susan said, her voice filled with a quiet resolve. "Generosity, hard work, and the joy of spreading happiness. It's more than just giving gifts—it's about making a difference in people's lives."

Sandy agreed, her eyes reflecting the warmth of the holiday decorations around them. "Yes, and I feel like we're just getting started. This experience has opened our eyes to so many possibilities. We've been part of something truly extraordinary, and it's left a lasting impression on our hearts."

With a deep sense of fulfillment and gratitude, the twins looked toward the future. They had been part of a remarkable journey, one that had enriched their understanding of Christmas and its true meaning. Eager to continue their path, they carried with them the lessons they had learned and the joy they had experienced.

As they prepared to leave the North Pole, they took one last look at the bustling workshop and the smiling faces of their friends. The warmth of the celebration and the magic of their adventure would stay with them, guiding them as they embarked on new journeys and embraced new opportunities.

With hearts full of hope and anticipation, Sandy and Susan stepped into the snowy landscape, ready to carry forward the spirit of Christmas and the joy they had shared with the world.

As the last of the celebration came to a gentle close, Sandy and Susan took one final, lingering look around the workshop. The once-bustling space was now quieter, but it was filled with a palpable sense of magic and possibility. The decorations, though slightly askew from the evening's festivities, still shimmered with holiday cheer. The twinkling lights and festive garlands, combined with the lingering echoes of laughter and music, were a testament to the hard work and dedication that had brought their mission to such a triumphant conclusion.

The twins stood side by side, their eyes taking in the scene with a mix of satisfaction and nostalgia. "It's hard to believe it's over," Sandy said softly, her voice tinged with awe. "This place has been our home for so long, and now it feels like a dream."

Susan nodded, her gaze lingering on the cozy corners of the workshop. "I know. It's been an incredible journey, and it's amazing to see the results of all our hard work. We've made a real difference, haven't we?"

The sense of accomplishment was evident in their smiles. Despite the challenges they had faced along the way, they had succeeded in their mission. The toys and furniture they had lovingly restored were now ready to bring joy to countless families. The knowledge that their efforts had contributed to such happiness filled them with pride.

With hearts brimming with joy and gratitude, Sandy and Susan embraced the future with a sense of hope and excitement. The magical journey they had experienced had deepened their understanding of Christmas and underscored the importance of bringing joy to others. It was more than just a mission; it was a revelation of the true spirit of the holiday season.

"This has been such a meaningful experience," Susan said, her voice steady with conviction. "It's shown us that Christmas is about much more than just gifts and decorations. It's about the love we share and the joy we bring to others."

Sandy smiled, her eyes reflecting the warm glow of the workshop. "Yes, and I feel like we're ready for whatever comes next. We've learned so much and have so much more to give. I'm excited to continue spreading this magic and making a difference wherever we go."

As they prepared to leave, they took one last look around, their hearts full of appreciation for the journey they had shared. The workshop, with its festive charm and the memories they had created, would always hold a special place in their hearts.

With a final wave and a shared, knowing smile, Sandy and Susan stepped into the snowy landscape, ready to embrace the future with open arms. Their adventure had been a testament to the power of Christmas magic, and they were eager to carry that magic forward, spreading joy and making the world a brighter and more joyful place.

As they walked away, the first light of dawn gently kissed the snow, signaling the start of a new day and new adventures. The twins felt a renewed sense of purpose and excitement, knowing that they were carrying with them the true spirit of the holiday season into all the possibilities that lay ahead.

EPILOGUE

The holiday season had come and gone, leaving behind a world transformed by the extraordinary efforts of two remarkable young women. As the first light of dawn crept across the snowy landscape of Grahamvale, Sandy and Suzie Casson awoke with a profound sense of fulfillment and peace. Their lives had changed in ways they could never have imagined, and the journey they had embarked upon had left an indelible mark on their hearts and the world around them.

The workshop, once a place of personal and familial heartbreak, had been reborn as a beacon of hope and joy. The grand building, decorated in festive hues and bustling with activity, was a testament to the twins' hard work and the magic they had embraced. What started as a humble mission to repair and deliver broken toys had grown into a thriving enterprise, one that brought smiles and laughter to countless children.

The twins had embraced their roles with enthusiasm and dedication. Each day, they worked alongside their team, including Elfin Toiz and other helpers who had joined them on their journey. The workshop was a hive of activity, filled with the sounds of laughter, the clinking of tools, and the occasional magical burst of energy. Their efforts had reached beyond Grahamvale, touching communities across North America and beyond. The toys and furniture they repaired had found new homes, spreading joy and enchantment wherever they went.

The reindeer, once a mere part of the magical lore they had encountered, had become a familiar sight in their daily operations. They had grown accustomed to the sight of the majestic creatures flying through the night sky, delivering gifts and spreading cheer. The sleds, painted in bright Christmas colors, had become symbols of the twins' commitment to their mission—a mission that went far beyond just repairing objects.

Santa Claus, or Nick as he was known to the twins, had become a cherished figure in their lives. His presence at the North Pole was a reminder of the magic that infused their work and the support that had guided them through their trials. The twins' bond with Nick had deepened, and their interactions were filled with warmth and mutual respect. They had come to understand the true essence of his role—not just as a figure of holiday cheer, but as a guardian of hope and a symbol of the belief that even the smallest acts of kindness could create ripples of change.

As Christmas morning arrived, Sandy and Suzie took a moment to reflect on their journey. They stood at the window of their workshop, watching the snowflakes drift lazily to the ground. The town of Grahamvale, bathed in the soft glow of the early morning light, seemed peaceful and serene. It was a stark contrast to the tumultuous times they had faced, but it was also a testament to the strength and resilience they had discovered within themselves.

Their hearts swelled with gratitude as they thought of the people who had supported them along the way—the friends, the community, and the magical beings who had become part of their extended family. They remembered the struggles they had faced and the lessons they had learned, and they felt a profound sense of accomplishment. The road had been long and challenging, but it had also been filled with moments of joy, discovery, and connection.

In the quiet of the morning, the twins knew that their journey was far from over. Their work was ongoing, and their mission to spread joy and hope would continue. They had built something that was more than just a business; they had created a legacy—a legacy of kindness, resilience, and the belief that magic exists in the everyday moments of life.

As they prepared to embark on another day of work, they felt a renewed sense of purpose. The future was bright, and they were ready to face it with the same courage and optimism that had carried them through their darkest times. The world was full of possibilities, and they were eager to explore them, knowing that their efforts would continue to make a difference.

And so, as the sun rose higher in the sky, Sandy and Suzie Casson set forth with a sense of joy and determination. They were no longer just two young women navigating a world of magic and mystery—they were symbols of hope, bearers of a legacy, and creators of a brighter, more magical future. Their story had come full circle, but the adventure was far from over. With each passing day, they would continue to bring light and joy to the world, carrying forward the lessons they had learned and the magic they had embraced.